"You are so beautiful. I've wanted you for so long."

"If you did, you hid it well from me," she pointed out helplessly.

"I've surrendered...I can't hide it anymore."

Flora's mouth ran dry. Clad in silk boxers that defined more than they concealed, Angelo was an intimidating sight for a woman who was still a virgin. Of course, that was not a truth she was eager to brandish. Her lack of experience was more an accident of fate than a deliberate choice, for she had not got close enough to consider intimacy with anyone since her engagement had been broken off three years earlier.

"I'm not beautiful," she told him almost defiantly, unwilling to trust him or any man.

Angelo suddenly smiled, and his lean dark face lit with a brilliance that made her heartbeat pick up speed as he came down beside her on the bed. "I think you are, and I'm only interested in my own opinion."

SECRETLY PREGNANT…
CONVENIENTLY WED!

With this ring, I claim my baby!

The amazing new trilogy by
bestselling Harlequin Presents® author

Lynne Graham

The charming and pretty English village of Charlbury
St. Helens is home to three young women whose
Cinderella lives are about to be turned upside
down…by three of the wealthiest, most handsome
and impossibly arrogant men in Europe!

Jemima, Flora and Jess aren't looking for love,
but all have babies very much in mind. Jemima
already has a young son, Flora is hoping to adopt her
late half sister's little daughter,
and Jess just longs to be a mom.

But whether they have or want a baby, all the girls
must marry ultimate alpha males to keep their
dreams—and Alejandro, Angelo and Cesario are not
about to be tamed!

SECRETLY PREGNANT…CONVENIENTLY WED!

Jemima's Secret—March
Flora's Defiance—April
Jess's Promise—May

Lynne Graham

FLORA'S DEFIANCE

TORONTO NEW YORK LONDON
AMSTERDAM PARIS SYDNEY HAMBURG
STOCKHOLM ATHENS TOKYO MILAN MADRID
PRAGUE WARSAW BUDAPEST AUCKLAND

Recycling programs
for this product may
not exist in your area.

ISBN-13: 978-0-373-12981-2

FLORA'S DEFIANCE

First North American Publication 2010

Printed in U.S.A.

FLORA'S
DEFIANCE

CHAPTER ONE

ANGELO VAN ZAAL studied the nine-month-old child that the nurse had brought to him. The little girl was golden-haired with the wide, pansy-blue eyes of a china doll, and the minute she saw him she smiled in happy recognition. The innocence of that trusting smile cut Angelo as sharply as a knife, for few children could have been subjected to a tougher start in life than little Mariska. Only a dark bruise and a scratch on one cheek bore witness to the fact that she had been miraculously thrown clear in her special car seat from the accident in which both of her parents had died.

'I understand that you are not related by blood to Mariska,' the female doctor by his side remarked.

'Her father, Willem, was my stepbrother, but I thought of him as my brother and I treated him as such,' Angelo stated with the clarity for which he was famed in the business world. 'I consider Mariska to be part of my family and I'm keen to adopt her.'

'The social worker in charge of her case did mention that you have been involved in Mariska's life since she was born—'

'I did what I could to support Willem and his wife, Julie. I only wish it had been enough,' he imparted with a wry twist of his mouth, as he knew that the medical staff would be well aware of the state in which Mariska's parents had been at the time of the crash. He was merely grateful that the sordid truth had not appeared in the newspapers.

Angelo van Zaal was an extraordinarily handsome man, the doctor reflected with an appreciative glance. He was also extremely wealthy, the bearer of a name famous for its benevolence in the field of philanthropy. Nevertheless, the steel magnate was equally well known for his ruthless cutting edge and success as a businessman. According to the press, a procession of international fashion models entertained him outside working hours. In looks, he had inherited his Spanish mother's black hair and darker skin tone rather than his Dutch father's fair colouring. But his eyes were a bright burning blue, as lucid as a flawless sapphire and enhanced by a frame of lush ebony lashes that gave his gaze spectacular impact. Tall, at several inches over six feet, and well built, he had attracted a good deal of notice from female staff and patients alike as they walked through the hospital to the children's ward. He was also, as far as the doctor was aware, still a single man.

'The hospital has had several enquiries about Mariska's welfare from her aunt, Flora Bennett. I understand that she is Julie's older sister.'

Angelo's superb bone structure took on a forbidding aspect. At the same time, he had a mental flash of eyes the colour of emeralds, skin as impossibly white as milk and the sort of lush full pink mouth that could plunge a man into an erotic daydream. Flora was a tall, feisty redhead with the kind of sensual appeal that would have entrapped a less wary and experienced male. As he had on previous occasions, Angelo crushed that provocative thought and shook himself free of it in exasperation. 'A half-sister,' he pronounced quietly. 'She and Julie had the same father.'

Angelo could have said a great deal more but he compressed his lips, reluctant to voice his hostility towards the other side of Mariska's family because that was a private matter. He'd had the then pregnant Englishwoman Julie Bennett and her connections investigated when Willem had decided to marry her, and his strong reservations about Julie had proved prophetic.

Had it not been for Julie's inclinations, Angelo was convinced that Willem would still be alive and, from what he had learned about Julie's elder sister at the same time, she was not to be trusted either. The same investigation had revealed that lurid scandal laced Flora's background; some years earlier she had used sleazy tactics in an attempt to advance and enrich herself in the workplace. While Flora was considerably more memorable in looks and personality than her rather more ordinary sister, she was an already proven gold-digger and Angelo knew he would go to any lengths to ensure that Willem's daughter, Mariska, was protected from her influence. Mariska would, after all, inherit her father's trust fund. As Willem had died before he'd reached the age where he could gain access to the money, his daughter would some day be a rich young woman.

Indeed, if Angelo had anything to do with the matter, Mariska would lead a very different life from that of either of her feckless parents. His wide sensual mouth hardened. He might have failed to rescue Willem from his demons, but doing the very best he could for his stepbrother's daughter would help him to sleep a little more peacefully at night.

The doctor cleared her throat as Mariska lay in Angelo's arms; he had been granted temporary custody of the child. 'Have you any plans to marry?' she enquired, unable to stifle her curiosity on that score.

Brilliant blue eyes flew straight to her blushing face. Angelo was too much of a player to reveal his thoughts but tension held him fast. 'It is possible,' he responded. 'Where this little girl is concerned, I still have much to think through.'

His acknowledgement that there might be some grounds for concern over his suitability as a single parent made the doctor give him an approving appraisal. Someone had once called Angelo van Zaal chilly but, although she would never have called him an emotional personality, he was innately practical and reliable. Many men would have shrugged off the problems of so troublesome a set of relatives, but Angelo had stood his ground and done what he could to help until the inevitable tragic end was reached. In the doctor's book, that not only made him a force to be reckoned with but also a very suitable guardian for a vulnerable child.

Flora sat rigid-backed in the taxi that had collected her from her flight into Schipol airport. Every step of her journey to Amsterdam had been organised without any input from her and, although those arrangements had made the trip easier for her, she was not only ungrateful for that assistance, but also as tense as a bowstring.

At five feet eleven inches tall, she was a long-limbed

coltish beauty with slender curves in elegant keeping with her height and graceful carriage. But Flora had never seen herself in that favourable light because from an early age she had been made to feel excessively large and gawky beside her dainty, diminutive mother who had often bemoaned her daughter's size.

Her thick auburn hair, which when loose fell well past her shoulders since she had decided to grow it again, was tied back with a black ribbon at her nape. Her apple-green eyes shone clear against her flawless skin, but the swollen reddened state of her eyelids betrayed the physical signs of her grief.

The knowledge that she would soon have to thank Angelo van Zaal for arranging her trip to Amsterdam for the double funeral made Flora grimace. She loathed him: he was such a controlling seven-letter-word of a man! His word was law within his family circle, at his offices and even beyond those boundaries, for such wealth as his carried considerable power and influence in every sphere. Flora, of course, had never liked being told what to do. She had learned to put up with it when she was an employee. She had also learned to keep her temper around bossy guests at her guest house, to nod and smile and let their arrogance wash off her again like a light rain shower.

But Angelo van Zaal could put Flora's back up without even trying. He had not even had the courtesy to phone her personally when her sister and his stepbrother had died within hours of crashing their car, she reflected bitterly. Instead he had instructed his family lawyer to ring and break the news for him. It was a dispassionate decision that was typical of his determination to keep her at arms length from events, thereby underlining his own authority and the absence of a true familial connection between them.

But if she was honest—and Flora always liked to be honest with herself—her primary objection to Angelo van Zaal was that, at first glance, he had turned her head as easily as if she were a dizzy adolescent. Even though eighteen months had passed since that debilitating first encounter, her cheeks could still burn at the mere memory of the effect he had on her—in spite of the fact that a man like Angelo van Zaal would never give her so much as a second glance.

Angelo was undeniably drop-dead gorgeous and Flora found it a terrible challenge not to stare at him and just float off into fantasy land. He flustered her and made her blush and stammer and, no matter how hard she tried to suppress her responses, she was already on the edge of her seat with anticipation at just the thought of seeing him again. There was no rhyme or reason to sexual attraction, she reminded herself impatiently. But all the same it exasperated her that even after her past unhappy experiences with men she could still succumb to a meaningless physical reaction. In truth, she was convinced that if sexual weakness could be inborn she had undoubtedly inherited that dangerous flaw from her womanising father. The acknowledgement that she could be drawn to someone she didn't even like shocked and affronted her, but she would have chewed off her own arm sooner than give Angelo van Zaal reason to suspect her weakness for him.

Furthermore, Angelo was severely underestimating her if he imagined that she might be willing to stand back and just allow him to claim full custody of her niece. Flora was ready to fight for the right to take Mariska back to England with her so that she could raise Julie's child as her daughter. Why should Angelo automatically assume that he would make the most appropriate guardian for a baby girl?

After all, Flora owned a comfortable detached house with a garden in the English village of Charlbury St Helens and was in a position to offer her niece her care and attention. At present, Flora, who also had a child-care qualification, ran a successful bed and breakfast business from her home. But, if need be, she could stop taking in paying guests until Mariska was of an age to attend school. Financially she could handle that temporary sacrifice of earnings because she had a good deal of money sitting untouched in the bank. She might not like to think about where that money had come from and what she'd had to go through to get it, but the very fact of its existence surely had to improve her chances of being considered a suitable adoptive parent.

As Flora detached herself from the disturbing memories of the very different life she had led as a city career woman before she'd settled into her former great-aunt's home in the village, she was painfully conscious of the ache of loss in her heart. Julie was gone and, sadly, Flora had seen all too little of her vivacious younger sister since she'd moved to the Netherlands. She had only seen Willem and Julie when they'd come over to the UK. Only once had Flora contrived to visit them in Amsterdam, for Willem and Julie had led very busy lives and it had quickly become apparent to her that they'd preferred to be guests rather than hosts.

Yet once upon a time Flora and the sibling five years her junior had been very close, although nobody who'd known the background from which both young women had come would ever have forecast that development. Flora had grown up as an only child in an unhappy marriage. Her father had been a chronic womaniser and she had few childhood memories that did not include a background of raised voices and the sound of her mother sobbing. Her emotionally fragile parent had often intimated that she would leave her unfaithful husband if only she could afford to do so, a lament that had ensured that her daughter set out to gain the highest possible educational qualifications in the hope of ensuring that she never had to rely on a man to keep a roof over her head.

Flora's parents had finally divorced while she'd been at university and she had then withstood the shock discovery that her father already had a second family, living only a few streets away from her childhood home! Evidently he had carried on an affair with Julie's mother, Sarah, almost from the outset of his marriage to Flora's mother. Her father had married Sarah straight after the divorce and there had been a huge family row when he'd insisted on introducing his daughters to each other. Even when that second marriage had also broken down in a welter of accusations of infidelity, Flora and Julie had stayed in touch, and when Julie's mother had died and Julie started college she'd moved into Flora's apartment in London. During the following two years, which had encompassed a period of great upheaval and unhappiness for Flora at work and in her personal life, the sisters had become close.

Flora's eyes swam with tears while she allowed herself to picture her late sister as she had last seen her. A small pretty blonde, Julie had been bubbly and chatty. Within months of meeting Willem, who had spent his gap year working in London, Julie had decided to abandon her studies so that she could live on a houseboat in Amsterdam with the handsome young Dutchman. Rejecting all Flora's cautious advice to the contrary, Julie had put love first with the wholehearted determination of the very young. Within weeks she had announced her pregnancy and soon afterwards a rather hasty marriage had taken place.

Angelo van Zaal had paid for the civil wedding and the small reception that had been held in London. Flora had only met him for the first time that day and, already warned what to expect from him by her sister, she had not been impressed by his chilly disapproval.

'I'm too common for Angelo's taste, not well enough educated and too cheeky for a woman,' Julie had told her with a scornful toss of her pretty blonde head. 'Catch me standing saying, "Yes, sir, no, sir, three bags full, sir" like Willem does! Willem is terrified of him because he's never managed to measure up to Angelo's expectations.'

And to be fair to Angelo van Zaal, he had made no attempt to pretend that he approved of her sister's relationship with his stepbrother. 'They're far too young and immature to be parents. This is a disaster,' he had pronounced with grim insensitivity after the ceremony, staring down at Flora with cold-as-ice blue eyes.

'It's a little late now,' Flora had countered, being of a naturally more optimistic bent, while marvelling at the unearthly beauty and unusual hue of those eyes of his. 'They do love each other and, thank goodness, they'll have Willem's trust fund to help them along—'

Angelo's lean bronzed face had frozen. 'Where did you get that idea from? Willem won't come into his trust fund for another three years.'

Flora had felt her face flood with mortified colour and wished she had kept her mouth shut. Was it wrong of her to have assumed that early access to the bride-groom's nest egg would provide much-needed help to the young couple in setting up their first home? The disdain on Angelo's handsome face had warned her that, as far as he was concerned, she had grossly overstepped her boundaries in referring to Willem's future prospects.

'I understand that they're both hoping that in the circumstances—Julie expecting their first child,' Flora had extended uncomfortably, 'they can challenge the provisions of the fund—'

'It would be insanity. I will not allow it,' Angelo had decreed in a tone of sardonic finality as though his opinion was the only one that counted. 'Willem and his wife will have to work for a living. Clearly that was not your sister's plan.'

Flora had bridled at the insinuation that her sister might have married Willem in the hope of sharing his handsome trust fund. 'Of course Julie is willing to get a job.'

'She's not qualified to do anything other than the most menial work,' Angelo had pointed out drily. 'And Willem will have to complete his business degree before he can aspire to a well-paid career.'

Ultimately the trust fund had been kept safe but what

Flora had most feared from the outset had come to pass
instead: Willem had dropped out of university to seek
employment when Julie had become too sick to work
during her pregnancy. Flora had blamed Angelo van
Zaal entirely for that development, believing that as one
of the trustees for the fund he had probably still patted
himself on the back for having kept that precious money
intact. She was not at all surprised that the steel billionaire had put the conservation of cash ahead of family
concern and kindness.

The taxi waited for her while she checked into her
hotel and then whisked her on to the funeral home. By
the time she arrived there she was truly dreading her
approaching encounter with Angelo van Zaal. There
was a large gathering of mourners, many of them young
people. But in spite of the crowd the only person Flora
was really aware of strode across the room towards her
and his very presence in the same airspace made her
light up inside like a secret firework display. Her spine
rigid with shame and denial, she blanked him out as
though he weren't there, evading any form of eye contact
while warm colour began to infiltrate her pallor.

Angelo spoke the conventional words of regret with
perfect courtesy, awaited her response and escorted
her round the room to meet some of Willem's relatives.
When it came to public behaviour his manners were
always letter perfect. But, so close to him, Flora could
hardly breathe for tension and she hated him for the
effect he was having on her, hated him for the lethal
combination of looks and hormones that had entrapped
her from their first meeting. Even the faint evocative
aroma of his citrus-based cologne was familiar to her

and she had to resist a powerful urge to lean closer to him. No man, even the one she had once planned to marry, had ever made such a strong impression on her.

Indeed, sex had never been a driving need for her and she was still a virgin. She had always been level-headed and reserved with men. She had seen too much unhappiness growing up to want to rush into any relationship. She had also once suffered badly from the harassment of a bullying sex-pest in the workplace. And the discovery of the potent physical attraction that Angelo, a man she didn't even like, could exude had merely underlined her caution and disenchantment with that aspect of life.

'How is Mariska doing?' Flora asked the moment she had the chance to speak to Angelo van Zaal without an audience.

'Children are resilient. She was all smiles over breakfast this morning,' Angelo recalled, staring down at her with his electrifyingly blue eyes, eyes unfairly surrounded by lashes as dense and enhancing as thick black lace.

'You saw her that early at the hospital today?' Flora pressed in surprise, thinking that he must have called in to see the little girl on his way to the funeral.

Angelo gazed down at her in an unnervingly steady appraisal and it was as if pure energy were dancing over her skin with silken taunting fingers. Tensing, alarmingly conscious that her nipples were tightening beneath her clothing, she coloured accordingly, stilled a shiver of awareness and stared fixedly at the knot on his silk tie.

'Mariska is no longer in hospital,' Angelo revealed. 'She was released into my care yesterday.'

That was news to Flora and she lifted her chin. 'You pulled that off very quickly. Who's looking after her?'

'Her nanny, Anke.'

Flora was unimpressed. 'When she's already lost her parents the company of a stranger can't be much of a consolation.'

'Anke is not a stranger. She has been taking care of Mariska on a part-time basis for several months now...'

'Willem and Julie employed a nanny?' Flora was taken aback, as she had not thought that the financial problems Julie had often mentioned during their phone calls would have stretched to such a luxury as one-to-one care for Mariska. And, certainly, Julie had never once hinted that her daughter enjoyed the attentions of Anke.

'I took care of the expense.' His wide sensual mouth compressed, Angelo dealt her a tough uncompromising look as though daring her to say more on yet another subject that he clearly considered to be none of her business.

'How very generous of you...as you have been in shelling out for my travel costs,' Flora commented stiffly. 'Thanks, but it wasn't necessary, though it did save me a lot of hassle and got me here much faster, which I do appreciate. I can't stay for long though, and I would like to spend what time I do have in Amsterdam with—'

'Your niece. Of course,' he incised smoothly. 'When this is over, everyone is invited back to my home for coffee and you'll see her then.'

Flora flushed, for she had not expected him to make

seeing Mariska so easy and had somehow expected obstacles to be put in her path. The wind taken from her sails before she even got airborne, she nodded relieved acceptance of his assurance.

'I should mention…' She hesitated and then pressed on, guided by her streak of innate honesty, which preferred all the facts to be out in the open. 'I have an interview with a solicitor here tomorrow and after that with Social Services. I intend to apply to adopt Mariska.'

All of a sudden, those impossibly blue eyes briefly resembled chips of indigo-tinted ice, but then she wondered if that was the result of her fertile imagination because he merely nodded his acceptance. 'Of course, that is your prerogative.'

The funeral did not last long. Someone had told her that the Dutch were partial to giving eulogies at funerals, but the tributes paid to Willem and Julie were short and sweet. Tears continually flooded Flora's eyes because it seemed so wrong that two such young people with everything to live for should be dead and she struggled to get a grip on emotions that still felt exceedingly raw. Apart from Mariska, Flora no longer had any surviving relatives and that made her feel very alone in the world. Her best friend, Jemima, had recently returned to her husband in Spain and that had left another hole in her life.

When the talking was over, Flora accepted a lift with Willem's aunt and uncle to Angelo's home. He lived in an imposing historic building, a literal mansion, which Julie had once described to Flora in the most fulsome of terms as a 'palace'. The house, which had belonged to several generations of van Zaals, was very traditional inside and out, featuring high ceilings, polished wooden floors, gleaming antique furniture and walls covered with huge splendid paintings. Coffee was served in the very elegant drawing room by the plump, smiling house-keeper whom Angelo addressed as Therese.

Under cover of a conversation with a business col-league, Angelo found himself discreetly watching Flora, noting her every tiny move and change of expression and the faint silvery sheen of tears still marking her cheeks. Even at a glance he could see that she seethed with emotion, messy dangerous stuff that it was, he ac-knowledged grimly, for she was the sort of woman he had always avoided getting involved with. More than a year had passed since their last meeting. He approved of the fact that her hair was no longer short and he could not resist picturing those luxuriant coppery tresses freed from the restraint of their ribbon. *And trailing across a pillow?* a sarcastic little inner voice enquired. As ir-ritation with his male predictability gripped Angelo, there was a tightening heaviness at his groin, his libido reacting all too enthusiastically to Flora Bennett's pres-ence and the allure of an erotic fantasy.

He sensed the passion in her and it drew him like the sun on a cold wintry day. Brilliant eyes cloaked, he studied her fixedly and, just as he had from their very first encounter, fought the magnetic pull of her with all his considerable force of will. Control and lucidity were everything to Angelo, who demanded more of himself than he ever had from anyone else. After all, nobody knew better than Angelo that an affair with the wrong woman could lead to disaster and it was the one risk he would not take.

Flora dragged her attention from a superb painting of an ancestral family group, striving not to seek Angelo's resemblance to some of its members with his clear good-looking features, though he would be like a sleek dark avenging angel set amongst those fair rosy-cheeked faces, she thought absently. She turned round to see where he was and collided headlong with his burning appraisal. An arrow of pure burning heat slivered through her slim length, kicking every nerve-ending into almost painful sensitivity. Her full lips pressed together tightly as she walked towards him, suppressing her responses with furious resolve.

Angelo inclined his handsome dark head to his housekeeper and summoned her to his side. 'Therese will take you upstairs now to see Mariska.'

Flora was introduced to the pretty dark-haired nanny, Anke, but she really only had eyes for her niece, who sat in a child seat playing with a selection of toys. With her slightly turned-up nose and dimples, blue eyes and golden hair, the little girl bore a startling likeness to Julie. Flora's eyes stung and she got down on her knees beside the chair to get reacquainted with her niece, once again deeply regretting the truth that she was almost a stranger to Mariska.

Mariska studied Flora with big blue eyes and laughed when her aunt tickled her chubby little hand. A cheerful, affectionate child, she played happily with Flora and she was the perfect comfort for her aunt after the highly stressful week she had endured. When the little girl became sleepy, Flora checked her watch and was surprised by how much time she had spent with her niece, for the afternoon was over. Descending the stairs, she saw Angelo in the hall below. He was so tall and dark and his glossy black cropped hair shone beneath the lights. He had the bronzed profile of a Greek god and the body of one as well, her rebellious thoughts added defiantly.

'I wondered if it would be possible for me to visit the houseboat where Willem and Julie lived tomorrow afternoon,' she asked tautly.

'Yes. A cleaning crew is currently sorting the vessel out for a handover back to the landlord,' Angelo revealed. 'There may be some of your sister's things which you wish to take home with you.'

There was a thickness in Flora's throat. Julie had always travelled light so she doubted that there would be many keepsakes. She forced a rather watery smile and took her leave to walk out into the cool evening air.

Watching her departure from the window, Angelo had the cold comfort of knowing that he was behaving badly. Flora was on her own in a foreign city and she had just buried her sister and her brother-in-law. Yet he was leaving her to return to an anonymous hotel for the evening. His handsome mouth clenched hard. Even as he watched her he noticed the enticing feminine sway of her hips in the dark suit she wore, the pouting curve of her bottom that stretched the skirt's fabric and the shapely turn of her calves and narrow ankles. She had terrific legs. He imagined inching up that skirt and as his body reacted with full blown arousal he released his breath in a sudden sharp hiss. He knew that he could not trust himself if he offered dinner and so left it at that.

Exhaustion engulfed Flora by the time she reached her room as she had barely slept since receiving the news of the double tragedy. She kicked off her shoes and lay down on the bed, where she fell asleep almost instantly. The chirrup of the phone by the bed wakened her. 'Hello?' she mumbled drowsily.

'It's Angelo.' It was an unnecessary announcement because Flora knew only one male possessed of a dark deep drawl as rich and potentially sinful as chocolate melting on her taste buds. 'Have you dined yet?'

Flora froze in surprise and wondered if he could hear the sound of her jaw dropping in shock. 'Er...'

'If you haven't I would be happy to take you out to eat this evening,' Angelo murmured, smooth as silk.

His voice actually set up a chain-reaction quiver down her taut spine and she sat up with a start. She could not credit the invitation and it unnerved her. 'Thanks, but I've already eaten,' she lied without hesitation. 'But it was kind of you to offer.'

'I wasn't being kind,' Angelo countered, a rougher edge filtering through his unforgettable drawl.

'Oh...' Dry-mouthed and flushed, Flora could not think of a single thing to say and he filled in the silence with complete cool and bid her goodnight. He didn't like her, she *knew* he didn't like her, for the cool censure when he looked at her with those amazing eyes of his was unmistakeable, even if she didn't know what she had done to deserve that attitude. So why on earth had he suddenly decided to invite her out to dinner? Had he felt sorry for her? The very suspicion made Flora bridle because she had never sought out any man for comfort.

She ordered a snack from Room Service and then went for a quick shower. She ate perched cross-legged on the bed with a book propped open and just knew that Angelo would disapprove. But she had said no and she should be proud of herself, although if she was honest panic and surprise had together combined to ensure her negative response. In addition she had nothing to wear but the suit she had worn to the funeral, since she had only packed casual jeans and a top for her short stay. She could not even imagine dining out in some fancy restaurant in Angelo's company. On her final visit to Charlbury St Helens, Julie had shown her sister a magazine article featuring a couple of Angelo's lady friends, beautiful women dressed in cutting-edge fashion, who could match his sophistication and cool.

Regardless of those reflections, Flora could not help wondering what it would have been like to be the sole focus of Angelo's attention for a couple of hours. Heat bubbled like excitement low in her pelvis and she tensed and suppressed that disturbing line of thought. It was a very long time before she contrived to drift off to sleep again that night…

CHAPTER TWO

THE following day, Angelo was in a business meeting in Rotterdam. But for all the attention he was giving to the exchange of views, he might as well have stayed at home. He was proud of his cool logic and intelligence and could not understand why both had proved insufficient to forecast Flora Bennett's most recent move. The dinner invitation had offered him a valid way of bringing Flora up to speed on events in her late sister's life before she got the bad news from the professionals she was consulting that very morning. It would have been tasteless for him to pass on that information at the funeral. But she had, most unexpectedly, turned him down.

Handsome mouth tightening and quite unaware of the attention his unusually long silence was attracting, Angelo shrugged a broad shoulder sheathed in the finest silk and wool mix. He was willing to admit that he had no prior experience of hearing the word 'no' from a woman's lips. It was a fact that the females he met fell over themselves to say yes. Yes to every invite, yes to sex, yes to just about any damned thing he wanted. Women in Angelo's world were very predictable and he had never had the smallest urge, he told himself fiercely, to walk on the wilder side of life. He had never forgotten the years of misery that had resulted from his late father's desire to do exactly that with Willem's mother, a beautiful volatile widow.

But would Flora have slept with him last night? That question came out of nowhere at him before he was even aware of having thought about such a possibility. He was impervious to the covert looks he was receiving as his brilliant blue eyes became even more abstracted. He wanted her. He was even willing to admit that there was just something about Flora Bennett that grabbed him every time he saw her. Yet last night his intentions had been pure.

Of course it was entirely possible that Flora Bennett knew a great deal more about Willem and Julie's lifestyle than he had had cause to suspect. His lean strong features darkened at that idea. Flora had seen little of her sister since her wedding to Willem, but she could well have decided to give Julie and her problems a wide berth. Angelo had never had that option because the overwhelming need to protect Mariska from her parents' folly had repeatedly forced him to intervene. Unfortunately taking care of Mariska's needs would entail building some kind of an ongoing connection with the other side of her family. He might distrust Mariska's aunt but she was still the only blood relative the little girl had left alive. He could not ignore that bond or the fact that Flora had spent over two hours happily entertaining her niece and had inspired her nanny to remark that Mariska's English aunt was wonderfully natural with children.

How much weight would the professionals put on that bond or on so admirably maternal a demonstration?

Was he prepared to get married just to improve his own claim to the little girl? Angelo shifted uneasily in his seat. The prospect of only sleeping with one woman for the rest of his life appealed to him as much as a dose of poison. Of course he could make marriage more of a business arrangement and retain a certain amount of freedom, he reasoned bleakly. Many women would accept such conditions simply to become a van Zaal with access to a fleet of private jets, a luxurious array of international homes and a huge allowance to spend on designer clothes and jewellery. Angelo had learned very young that it was possible to buy virtually anything he wanted and he was prepared to pay handsomely over the odds to acquire the perfect wife.

A perfect wife who would naturally be blonde, educated, classy and from the Netherlands. Dutch women were wonderfully practical and resilient, he thought appreciatively. He needed a sensible woman from a respectable background who would accept his challenging work schedule without complaint and who would embellish his social and domestic life while still essentially allowing him his privacy. A woman content to enjoy the lifestyle he could give her and make no further demands of him. He decided that as long as the controversial subjects of fidelity or romance were kept off the menu he could face the prospect of marriage for Mariska's sake. He had become very fond of the little girl.

Emerging from that lengthy and very sobering thought process, Angelo checked his watch and made one of the lightning-fast decisions that he was famous for. After a working lunch to make up for his non-participation in the meeting, he would meet Flora Bennett at the houseboat and tie up the loose ends between them before she left Amsterdam and returned to England. It was the rational thing to do and he was not being influenced by his attraction to her, he assured himself with considerable satisfaction. He was far too level-headed to stray into such hazardous territory with a woman of dubious morals.

Around the same time as Angelo was travelling from his head office in Rotterdam back to Amsterdam, Flora was literally reeling out of the public building where she had met with Mariska's social work team: she was in deep shock from what she had learned during that encounter.

Shock that she'd had not the slightest idea of what really had gone on in Willem and Julie's lives, shock that Julie had managed to convince her during their weekly phone calls that they were leading a perfectly ordinary life when, in fact, the very opposite was true. Indeed, both Willem and her sister had resorted to petty crime in an effort to satisfy their addiction to drugs. Her half-sister and her husband had been *thieves and drug addicts*. Hopelessly addicted, so that despite all pleas and offers of counselling that had been offered to them they had continued on their dogged path to self-destruction. Indeed Willem and Julie had been high when Willem had crashed their car and then he and his wife had died. Flora remained amazed by the stroke of fate that had kept Mariska alive.

Although every attempt had been made to shield Angelo's privacy it had slowly become abundantly clear to Flora that Willem's stepbrother had been heavily involved from the outset in all attempts to persuade the young couple to enter a rehabilitation programme. He had also done everything that he could to protect his stepbrother's child from harm.

In recent months, Mariska had virtually never been left to rely on parental care alone. Either she had been in day care or in her nanny's care, and when Willem and Julie had partied and Anke had deemed her charge to be at risk she had taken Mariska to Angelo's home. Yet, even with all those safeguards in place, Flora's niece could still easily have been killed along with her parents when Julie had chosen to take her daughter out of day care early one afternoon without telling anyone and had got into Willem's car with her. Mariska's very survival was a small miracle.

A stiff late spring breeze gusted down the street of tall, narrow and highly ornamental buildings that bordered the canal Flora was walking alongside and her tears chilled on her cheeks. She stepped hurriedly out of the way of a cyclist riding past and sucked in a steadying breath while she paused to consult the map she had bought to help her negotiate the maze of streets.

It was an effort to think straight while she was being eaten alive by a great burst of angry resentment and regret. But her half-sister was gone and nothing could bring Julie back. Yet on whose say-so had Flora been excluded from knowing about and *trying* to help the young couple? Flora had a very strong suspicion about the identity of that culprit. While the social workers had been bound by rules of confidentiality, only Angelo van Zaal would have dared to leave Julie's one close relative in ignorance of her plight.

When she'd first moved to Amsterdam, Julie had sent her sister loads of photos, so now Flora had little difficulty picking out the bright blue-and-white-painted houseboat from the others moored on a quiet stretch of water overlooked by a picturesque terrace of gabled houses. After all, she had a framed sunlit picture of that same evocative scene sitting in her home. She stepped onto the deck and as she did so the door of the cabin opened, framing the tall black-haired male whose inexcusable silence over the past year had stoked her umbrage.

For an instant, Flora froze, her wide green eyes locking onto Angelo van Zaal. He looked strikingly elegant if out of place in his formality in a dark grey business suit and silk tie. The suit had the exclusive fit of a tailored designer garment, framing wide strong masculine shoulders and hugging lean hips and long muscular thighs. As he stepped outside the breeze ruffled his luxuriant black hair above his lean, darkly handsome features. The sheer impact of his physical charisma hit her like a sudden blow to the head, leaving her dizzy. She collided with sapphire-blue eyes and her tummy shimmied like a jelly while her breath feathered in her throat.

'What on earth are you doing here?' she demanded tautly.

'This seemed to be an opportune time and place to talk to you.'

'It's a little late for that now, isn't it?' Green eyes flashing as emerald as jewels in sunlight, Flora stalked past his tall still figure into the saloon of the houseboat. The spacious interior had a bare look, for all the surfaces were clear and a stack of cardboard boxes spread out from one corner. 'In fact I would say that talk of any kind between us now would be a waste of your valuable time.'

Unaccustomed to such a bold unapologetic attack, and with his handsome mouth in a sardonic line, Angelo studied her. Colourful copper-coloured hair falling in a lavish windblown cloud round her shoulders, Flora wore a short black trench coat, jeans and a green sweater, and even in that casual garb she looked amazing, he acknowledged with distinct reluctance. She had the transparent alabaster skin of the true redhead and soft pink self-conscious colour defined her cheekbones while he studied her, quietly marvelling at the amount of emotion she contrived to emanate even when she was silent. Trembling with the force of her fury, Flora undid her coat, dropped it down on a seat and spun back to face him.

'How could you not tell me what was going on here?' she demanded in ringing reproach. 'Willem and Julie were *my* family as well. At the very least I had a right to know that Julie was taking drugs!'

'She was an adult of twenty-one, Flora. She made her own choice, which was that under no circumstances were you to be told about their problems.'

Flora lifted her chin in challenge. 'Meaning?'

'Exactly what I said. I did speak to her and I know for a fact that her social worker urged her to confide in you, but your sister didn't want you to know that she had got caught up in drugs and I was not in a position to go against her wishes.'

'I don't believe that.' Flora dealt him a furious

unimpressed look, convinced that he was simply trying to palm her off with excuses. 'You always do as you like, Angelo. You're a strong man. You're no one's whipping boy!'

'Believe me when I tell you that it was a huge struggle to keep the communication lines between me and Willem and Julie open. Their lifestyle was abhorrent to me but for their daughter's sake it was imperative that I still retained access to them,' Angelo retorted grimly. 'Had I gone against your sister's wishes they would no longer have trusted me and Mariska would have suffered...'

'So you got involved and I was left on the outside, kept in ignorance of what was happening in Willem and Julie's lives until it was too late,' Flora condemned with unconcealed bitterness.

'I made Mariska's needs my priority,' Angelo countered without apology. 'I did the best I could in a very difficult situation.'

'Well, the best you could wasn't good enough, was it?' Flora threw at him fierily, her temper rising again like steam inside a kettle as the sheer awfulness of what she had learned that morning bit into her like painful claws on tender flesh. 'Less than a year after Mariska's birth, your stepbrother and my sister are both dead and their child is an orphan!'

His superb bone structure rigid, Angelo surveyed her with cool ice-blue, astonishingly clear eyes set above the smooth olive planes of his handsome face. His eyes had the shockingly vivid clarity of a glacier lake she had once seen in the Alps, she thought absently. It struck her that so far nothing she had said had moved him in the slightest and his rigorous self-control seemed to mock her emotional state.

'Willem and Julie were a fatal combination,' Angelo murmured in a tone of flat finality. 'Willem was weak and troubled, and before they even met Julie was a habitual drug user.'

As the ramifications of that accusation sank in, shocking Flora all over again, she released a jagged laugh of disbelief. 'How dare you try to blame Julie for what happened to them? How dare you insinuate that she was the prime instigator?'

'I am telling you what I know to be the truth. I have no desire to malign your memory of your sister.'

Flora shot him an enraged glance, green eyes luminous as green glass on the seashore. 'Then don't do it.'

'I did not hurl the first stone,' Angelo countered levelly, his attention wandering to the way the fine wool sweater lovingly moulded the small pouting curves of her breasts and defined the slight bump of her prominent nipples. He suspected that she wasn't wearing a bra and the full taut sensation of heaviness at his groin increased as he imagined peeling off that sweater. It took enormous self-discipline to wrench his mind back from that erotic reverie and her ability to distract him without even trying to do so infuriated him.

'You could have told me that Willem and Julie had got involved in drugs!' Flora slung at him in a seething undertone, her eyes bright with antagonism and accusation. The growing tension in the atmosphere only put her more on edge. 'And you could have told me that I had to conceal where I got that information from.'

'As I've already said, when I was unable to persuade either Willem or his wife to stop using drugs or even to enter counselling, my main goal was to protect Mariska from their excesses.'

Flora snatched in an audible breath in an effort to calm her teeming emotions down to a more controllable level. She folded her arms tightly and crossed the floor, her slender spine stiff as a pencil. The dreadful compulsion to stare at him had her in its hold, though, for when she looked once she always had to look back at him again and admire his amazing bone structure, dazzling eyes and tall, powerful physique. That he could stun her even in the midst of a bitter argument outraged her sense of what was decent. In measured rejection she fixed her eyes on the view of the quiet canal beyond the window. 'It's so unfair that you're trying to foist the blame on Julie.'

'I am not trying to do that,' Angelo rebutted, his attention jerking away from the snug fit of her jeans over her heart-shaped derrière, for his imagination had really not required that added stimulus in her radius. His susceptibility to her every move around him galled him and gave him a disturbingly unfamiliar sense of being out of control. 'But I must be honest with you, even if you find that honesty offensive.'

'It is deeply offensive that you should accuse my sister of having been an habitual substance abuser,' Flora pointed out thinly, turning back to him for emphasis while her tongue slid out to moisten the dry curve of her lower lip.

'Even if I know that to be true?' Instantly engaged in picturing the effect of that small pink tongue tip on a highly sensitive part of his own anatomy, Angelo surveyed the sultry raspberry-tinted fullness of her mouth with driven concentration. She was making him feel ridiculously like a sex-starved adolescent boy and his hands clenched into defensive fists by his side.

'How could you possibly *know* such a thing to be true?' Flora flung in angry, scornful dismissal of that claim. She clashed head-on with his electrifyingly blue eyes, which might as well have been lit by tiny blue flames for she had the sensation of heat dancing over her entire skin surface. She flushed and her nipples tingled almost painfully while a scratchy sensation of warmth and awareness settled between her legs. In an uneasy movement, she shifted position off one foot on to the other.

'I know because I had Julie privately investigated before she married Willem,' Angelo admitted with unapologetic gravity. 'As a student in London your sister was running with a druggie crowd and regularly took ecstasy and cocaine. Even though she was pregnant she brought those habits to Amsterdam with her and it wasn't long before my stepbrother joined her and the two of them began to experiment with heroin.'

As Angelo spoke Flora had fallen very still and her eyes were very wide and dark with dismay. 'You had Julie investigated? There must be some mistake?'

'There was no mistake,' Angelo told her steadily, noticing how pale she had become, noting too how that pallor merely accentuated her bright copper hair and lustrous green eyes. Even her prickly argumentative nature could not detract from her considerable appeal. 'The report was done by a reputable firm and it was very detailed. I'm afraid that even as a teenager your sister was a heavy user of recreational drugs—'

'It's not possible. When Julie was a student, she was living with me,' Flora confided, and her voice slowly trailed away as she took that thought to its natural conclusion and looked back in time, a sinking sensation forming in the pit of her stomach.

Unfortunately, Julie had moved into Flora's flat and started college during what was a very fraught period in her older sister's life. Flora had had to put in very long hours at work while being harassed by a bullying boss. She had also been struggling to keep a demanding fiancé happy and she had not been able to give her half-sister the time and attention that she would have liked. Even so, she valued her memories of their time together back then and had seen nothing in Julie's behaviour that might have suggested that there was anything seriously amiss in her life. Certainly Julie had enjoyed a very active social calendar, but then so did most students, Flora reasoned ruefully. She did recall the very late hours the younger woman had kept and Flora, who'd had to be at work early, had usually been asleep by the time her sister came home. Julie had also been very prone to changeable moods and staying in bed all day at weekends, but that kind of behaviour could surely be ascribed to many teenagers?

'If Julie took drugs in those days, and I'm not sure I can accept that that could be true,' Flora breathed abruptly and without warning discovered that her eyes were prickling with tears, 'I hadn't the slightest idea of what she was up to.'

Angelo, who had a conscience as tough as the steel

his factories manufactured, saw moisture shimmer in her beautiful green eyes and he closed the distance between them without even being aware of a prompting to do so. Bare inches away from her, he faltered to a halt and hovered, suddenly uncharacteristically uncertain of what to do next because he was a man who had always walked the other way or turned a blind eye when women got upset. But he stared down into her tear-wet face and in an action that felt ridiculously natural to him, but which was actually not at all his style, he reached for both her hands to hold them firmly within his.

'Don't cry,' he told her urgently. 'Don't blame yourself for this fiasco. Many well-intentioned and experienced professionals tried and failed to help Willem and Julie. Sometimes no matter what you do you can't change things. What happened to them is in no way your fault.'

And Flora recognised his sincerity and finally accepted that the sad tale he was telling her was indeed the truth as he knew it. Guilt cut through her, though, like a knife as her first thought was that she had failed her sister when Julie had needed her most. While they'd been living together, she should have realised that Julie had problems and watched over her more closely. She should have refused to accept the seemingly little white lies and excuses that, even then, she had suspected her sibling was prone to hiding behind and probed more deeply, asking the awkward prying questions that she had swallowed back for the sake of peace. In those days, Flora had been afraid to tax their new sibling bond by acting too much like a pseudo-parental figure. And tragically that dangerous desire to be liked and to seem younger and more hip had evidently ensured that Julie had been free to take the first fatal steps towards becoming a drug addict.

'Julie had such a h-horrible childhood!' Flora stammered chokily, unable to silence the words brimming to her lips in her need to defend her late sister from the bad opinion he must have formed of her. 'She used to see my father out shopping in town with Mum and I and she had to pretend she didn't know him, even though he was her father as well. His affair with her mother, Sarah, was a big secret and it meant that for years and years while Julie was growing up she had to live a lie. That background left scars, of course it did. She lived to be noticed, she craved love and attention—'

'It's not your fault, *querida*. You were not her mother. You had no control over her. What, realistically, could you have done to change anything?' Angelo replied soothingly, his dark deep drawl fracturing as he stared down into her tear-bright green eyes.

That close to his lean, powerful body, Flora could smell the distinctive scent of his skin, an intoxicating mixture of citrus overlaying husky male, and as she drank in that aroma it made her tremble. A little inner voice whispered caution, warned her to step back and keep her distance from him, but her feet might as well have been nailed to the floor. She could feel herself beginning to lean forward, her attention locked to those unforgettable features of his, memorising the high line of his patrician cheekbones, the stubborn strength of his jaw and the arrogant jut of his classic nose. He drew her like a rock in a violent storm at sea.

He bent his proud dark head and parted her lips with

his wide sensual mouth and it was as if she had been waiting all her life for that one kiss as it ran through her like a depth charge and struck deep in a sensual and potent explosion. Her hands flew up and clenched into his wide strong shoulders. It couldn't be him, she thought momentarily in wonderment, it couldn't *possibly* be Angelo van Zaal who was making her feel as though she were racing with her heart pounding on a wild roller-coaster ride. The pall of apprehensive isolation and loss that had dogged her since she had flown out to Amsterdam was suddenly banished.

One kiss led straight into the next and her fingers dug into his jacket for support to keep herself upright. Shaking, she felt a shudder rack his big powerful body against hers and she exulted in the hand he closed to her hip to press her into provocative contact with the hard swell of his erection. Something that had turned her off other men turned her on with him. The very knowledge that she aroused him went to Flora's head and because of what had happened in the past she gloried in that intoxicating proof of his masculine response to her. She was dizzy, exchanging feverish kisses while the passion exploded through her like a shot of brandy on an icy day. Heat sizzled through her veins and pooled low in her tummy. She discovered that she couldn't make herself let him go for long enough to catch her breath.

'You're wearing far too many clothes,' Angelo said thickly.

Flora looked up at him, revelling in the temperamental glimmer of stormy blue visible below his dense black lashes. She was amazed by the discovery that he was not one half as calm, cool and controlled as she had always believed. There was a wild hunger in that appraisal that gripped her imagination like a key to a locked door, promising her a glimpse of the unknown. Angelo was gorgeous, absolutely gorgeous, but until that heady moment of recognition he had always been a closed and forbidding book to her. Just then seeing him look at her as though she were the most desirable woman alive was balm to a self-esteem that had once been battered to pulp when the man she loved rejected her.

Her fingers slid from his shoulder down onto his shirt front, spreading starfish fashion on the muscular heat of his powerful chest. With a gruff sound in his throat his mouth swooped down on hers again with a dominant force that sent a primitive shiver of delight darting through her slender length. He pulled her back against him and eased a hand below her sweater to cup a small pouting mound topped by a swollen pink nipple. A gasp parted her lips below the marauding pressure of his mouth and his tongue darted deep in the moist interior. The effect of that driving passionate kiss, added to the effects of the blunt masculine fingers toying with the peaks of her breasts was more than she could bear and she sagged against him, her legs refusing to hold her up.

'Come here, *querida mia*,' Angelo growled, hauling her up into his arms without further ado and kissing her with passionate fervour…

CHAPTER THREE

THIRTY seconds later, Flora's lashes lifted. She was lying on a bed in a compact cabin. Her sweater had gone and, mortified by the sight of her bared breasts, she raised herself on her elbows ready to call time on the extraordinary event that was unfolding when she focused on Angelo.

He had already shed jacket and tie and his shirt hung open on a bronzed hair-roughened torso and the flat corrugated planes of his stomach. He looked amazing, every inch a male pin-up worthy of a centrefold. The oxygen Flora needed just vanished from her lungs without warning.

'How did this happen? We shouldn't be doing this...' she gasped breathlessly, suddenly thinking about the sister she had lost and mentally squirming away from that painful reminder to take refuge in the present again.

'*Dios mio*...don't ask me to stop, *querida*,' Angelo urged, blue eyes electrifyingly hot and hungry as they collided head-on with hers. 'I've never wanted any woman as much as I want you at this moment.'

Cheeks burning with self-consciousness, Flora hunched her shoulders and crossed her hands over her naked chest, embarrassed by the insubstantial size of her womanly curves, while her bemused thoughts were already replaying what he had just said. It shook her how good she felt being Angelo's object of desire and how much she liked the fact that he was unzipping his well-cut trousers with more haste than cool while seemingly unable to drag his gaze from her where she lay on the bed. In truth, she acknowledged in an instant of pure insight, any form of human contact and comfort eased the terrible bleak pain of the realization that she would never see her little sister again.

'You are so beautiful,' Angelo murmured in a dark deep voice that had a wonderfully distracting effect on her because she was desperate to avoid the desolate thoughts hovering on the horizon of her mind. 'I've wanted you for so long.'

'If you did you hid it well from me,' she pointed out helplessly.

'I've surrendered… I can't hide it any more.' Angelo stepped clear of the trousers and her mouth ran dry. Clad in silk boxers that defined more than they concealed, Angelo was an intimidating sight for a woman who was still a virgin. Of course that was not a truth that Flora was eager to brandish. Her lack of experience was more an accident of fate than a deliberate choice, for she had not got close enough to consider intimacy with anyone since her engagement had been broken off three years earlier.

'I'm not beautiful,' she told him almost defiantly, unwilling to trust him or any man.

Angelo suddenly smiled and his lean dark face lit up with a brilliance that made her heartbeat pick up speed as he came down beside her on the bed. 'I think you are and I'm only interested in my own opinion.'

When he smiled she felt as if she could fly, but Flora had no time for such fanciful thoughts and she was bone-deep stubborn, shrugging off the way he could make her feel to add in a tone of distinct challenge, 'I'm much too tall for a woman—'

'I'm tall and you're the perfect size for me,' Angelo countered, undaunted by her comeback as he joined her with predatory grace.

Men had always tended to find Flora too bluntly spoken for comfort but Angelo appeared to take that candour very much in his stride. He captured her hands in his so that she could no longer hide her body from him.

For a timeless moment she lay there while he caressed her wrists with his thumbs, his attention hotly pinned to the stiff crests of her prominent nipples. 'You have very pretty breasts,' he husked, intense blue eyes embellished by lush black lashes.

Embarrassment claimed her. She could not be comfortable lying there half naked in broad daylight. She shut her eyes tight and wondered what insanity had come over her and then he kissed her again and the insanity came back with a vengeance, blurring all rational thought and inhibition. Nothing had ever felt so sweet or so necessary to her as his mouth. His tongue plunged into the tender responsive interior of her mouth and lit her up inside like a fire. She had not known that much pleasure could exist in mere kissing.

Her hands sank into his black hair as he nibbled down the cord of her slender neck and began to centre his attentions on her swollen sensitive breasts. His tongue lashed over the tender tips before the graze of his teeth on her delicate flesh made her cry out and tremble while the burn of excitement travelled straight to the moist heat gathering at the heart of her body. He pressed the heel of his hand against the apex of her thighs and she writhed, helpless beneath that pleasure inflicted on the most sensitive part of her. She felt the zip give on her jeans, her hands falling from him as he sat up to remove the garment.

'This is crazy,' she muttered jaggedly, 'out of control.'

'I've never been out of control in bed before. It's exciting,' Angelo confided, pushing up her face with an impatient hand to steal another explosive kiss.

And when his hard, hungry mouth was sealed to hers, nothing mattered and nothing else existed. He cupped the damp crotch of her knickers and then whisked them off to explore the slick wet folds between her thighs. She was hyper-sensitive there and she dug her hips into the mattress beneath her and little sounds escaped her lips without her volition. Teasing the delicate entrance, he rubbed the tiny bud where all her nerve-endings centred. Drenched in exquisite waves of pleasure beyond any she had ever experienced, she became ever more frantic. A sense of pressure was building in her tummy and a pulsing ache stirred between her legs, making her feel unbearably taut and needy.

Angelo slid between her thighs. She looked up at him with apprehensive green eyes, reacting to the probing feel of him against her most intimate place. He shifted and sank into her, stretching her hot tight channel with his girth and length. His hungry growl of pleasure masked her hastily swallowed huff of pain as he thrust past her resisting flesh and filled her to the hilt.

'You're so tight you feel incredible,' Angelo groaned, blue eyes radiating deep sensual satisfaction as he gripped her hips in hard hands and moved slowly and erotically, acquainting her with the full extent of his power.

Instinct made her arch her spine and rise up as he withdrew and slammed back into her in a pagan rhythm that made her every sense sing. Her body wasn't her own any more. Invaded and controlled by his driving urgency and her own need to answer its demands, she was overwhelmed by the thunderously exciting rise of pleasure. The pressure built and built to a nerve-racking high inside her. She squirmed and writhed in the last seconds before an explosive orgasm ripped through her trembling body like an earthquake, sending sweet shards of ecstatic pleasure shooting through every limb.

Afterwards she was drained and wrapped in a cocoon of exhaustion. He gazed down at her, blue eyes shimmering, and he kissed her again, slow and deep and hungry. *Hungry?* He was ready to do *it* again. She wasn't and was taken aback by his energy. Animation was returning to her brain and suddenly she wanted a magic lamp to rub so that she could leap fully clothed onto the quay beyond the window and run away as fast as her cowardly legs could carry her. What was she doing? Oh, what had she done, *what…had…she…done?* Bewilderment and shame drenched her in a tidal wave of regret. Her arms were wrapped tightly round him and she whipped them off him at supersonic speed and jerked free of his embrace.

'I've got to go,' she told him shakily. 'Places to go, people to see.'

Wincing at that airhead announcement even as it fell from her lips, Flora scrambled off the bed with a haste she couldn't hide.

Startled by her abrupt flight from his arms, Angelo pushed himself up on his elbows and rested frowning dark blue eyes on her. 'What's up?'

Stark naked, wreathed in blushes and with not the smallest idea where the bathroom was, Flora hovered in horrible confusion. What's up? she almost screeched back at him. Are you that insensitive that you think this situation, this appalling misstep, could possibly be acceptable?

'This should never, ever have happened. I'm embarrassed!' Flora gasped, reckoning he needed it all spelled out in simple words so that he could understand normal human reactions.

'Why should you be embarrassed? What we just shared was amazingly good sex,' Angelo commented thickly, pushing his powerful bronzed shoulders back against the tossed pillows and surveying her with deeply appreciative sapphire-blue eyes. 'Come back to bed.'

Every bit of Flora that wasn't already blushing took on a scarlet hue. *Come back to bed?* Whoever had said that men had a one-track mind had not been joking! Through an open door she espied something that looked reassuringly like a plumbing fixture and she sped towards it without further ado, only to discover that she was in what appeared to be a closet lined with pipes.

The door opened. Angelo looked in at her, alarmingly tall and broad and graphic in the nude. 'The bathroom is across the passage.'

Her hands knotted into fists. She was so upset she marvelled that she wasn't having a heart attack. On the way past the bed again she bent to scoop up her discarded clothes, trying not to wince at the soreness lingering between her thighs. Her first sex ever and she wanted to forget it, she thought in anguish. In the tiny bathroom she washed as best she could. There were no towels, just as there had been no bedding. She had rolled about on a bare mattress with Angelo van Zaal like a cheap slut and the mortification of that unacceptable fact bit deep.

A knock sounded on the door and she opened it a reluctant crack. 'Yes?'

'I have a country house. I'd like you to spend the weekend there with me,' Angelo suggested smoothly.

'Was the sex *that* good?' Flora enquired in a frozen voice that would have chilled a polar bear.

'I don't do one-night stands,' Angelo drawled softly.

Flora was getting desperate. 'Why don't you just go back to your office or whatever and leave me here?'

'We'll talk when you come out.' There was just the hint of a rougher edge to his tone as if he was finally accepting that she didn't even want to speak to him, never mind look at him, after the intimacy they had shared.

At least Angelo hadn't guessed that she had been a virgin until he touched her, Flora reflected wretchedly as she struggled back into her crumpled clothing in the confined space. Somehow the thought of Angelo van

Zaal, with his stable of glossy, sophisticated supermodel girlfriends, learning that she had been a sad twenty-six-year-old virgin struck her as the final humiliation. He would think she had been desperate for a man to show an interest in her and that wasn't how she was at all. Flora just didn't have a very high opinion of men and didn't think that a man was always necessary to a happy life. After her broken engagement she had stopped dating and had concentrated her energy on rebuilding her life.

As she emerged from the compartment Angelo appeared in the bedroom doorway to direct her back upstairs. She recalled him carrying her to bed and kissing her every step of the way and her pale skin flushed a deep rosy pink. How on earth could she have behaved that way? She was a very private person and she had standards, strict standards. Casual sex was anathema to her and what for him had probably just featured as an excitingly unexpected roll between the sheets with an almost stranger meant a great deal more to her in terms of pride and self-respect.

Angelo watched Flora dig her feet into her shoes and reach for her coat. She was behaving as if she could not get away from him quickly enough, a reaction very far removed from what he usually received from women in the aftermath of intimacy, and her unashamedly dismissive attitude set his even white teeth on edge.

At the same time an unusual sense of dislocation was assailing Angelo, as if his world had suddenly been turned upside down and everything felt wrong and out of place. In the circumstances, it was hardly surprising that Angelo, always so in control of events and of himself, was in deep shock. He had, after all, just engaged in unprotected sex for the first time in his life. Even the awareness that he did not have a condom had failed to stop him in his tracks. He had gone way beyond the age when he always carried protection, for not since he'd been a teenager had he engaged in an impetuous sexual encounter. Yet he had knowingly accepted the risk he was running and had found Flora so irresistible that he had taken her regardless of all common sense. Those acknowledgements shattered many of the convictions Angelo had long held about his own character. What the hell had come over him?

'Are you using any form of contraception?' Angelo asked flatly.

Flora's head flew up, green eyes unguarded and full of dismay as she frowned, following that question back to its logical source only to register that neither of them had considered that possibility at the time. 'No, I'm not… Are you saying that—?'

'This—what just transpired between us,' Angelo extended with a shift of fluid brown hands that was very Mediterranean and non-verbally eloquent, reminding Flora that her sister had once mentioned that he had had a Spanish mother. 'It was out of character for me.'

'And for me,' Flora muttered numbly, tying the belt on her coat and pulling it tighter than was comfortable, desperately needing to keep her hands busy.

'I didn't stop to think of consequences. We had sex without protection, which was very foolish of both of us. However, I have regular health checks and you need have no fear of disease. *But*—'

Flora was already settling aghast eyes on him and she

said shakily before he could continue, 'Obviously there's still a risk that you might have got me pregnant.'

'Let's try to be optimistic. We only had sex once and for all that we know one of us could even be infertile. We'll have to hope that the odds are in our favour,' Angelo breathed with deliberate cool, convinced that since he had never before tempted fate he would surely get away with it. He refused to even consider the alternative because messy situations like unplanned pregnancies had no place in his perfectly organised life.

Flora was stunned by his optimistic outlook, for she was much more prone to worrying that any moral mistake automatically attracted a punishment.

'As it's obvious that you don't want me to stay,' Angelo remarked silkily, one lean brown hand resting on the door, 'I'll leave you here to sort through those boxes.'

Flora had dug her hands into her pockets. 'Right. Okay,' she said awkwardly. 'I'd like to see Mariska again before I leave Amsterdam.'

Cool blue eyes rested on her anxious face. 'You're welcome to visit her whenever you like.' He reached into his pocket to withdraw a pen and write on the back of a business card. 'This is my home telephone number if you want to make arrangements with Anke.'

Flora studied the card he handed her with fixed attention, reluctant to look at him again. The atmosphere was so raw with unspoken tension that it squeezed at her nerves and her ability to breathe normally.

'I'll be in touch,' Angelo drawled.

Immediately, Flora braved her demons to glance up at him. 'That's not necessary,' she told him woodenly.

'We need to stay in contact for Mariska's sake,' Angelo contradicted. 'I will also seek reassurance that you are not pregnant. When will you know?'

Flora reddened at that very personal question. 'Mind your own business!'

Angelo dealt her a stony look shot through with re-inforced steel. 'If you conceive my child, it will be very much my business, *querida*.'

As soon as he was gone, having told her where to leave the key when she was finished, Flora shed her coat again and embarked on the first box. Mariska in mind, she set Julie's diaries and photographs to one side along with a rather battered teddy that her sister had once kept on her bed. There was not much else to be conserved aside from a few cards exchanged between Willem and Julie and some inexpensive costume jewel-lery that she thought her niece might one day like to look at. She studied the photo of Willem and Julie on their wedding day, so young, so happy and full of innocent hope, and a flood of tears overwhelmed her. She wept until she was empty, and although her throat was sore afterwards, she felt much better for having vented her emotions. She then made use of the phone number that Angelo had given her and organised a time to visit that afternoon and see Mariska.

In the little bathroom she splashed her swollen eyes with cold water and thought she looked an absolute sight. She still could barely credit that she had had sex with Angelo van Zaal. Were there more of her sexu-ally adventurous father's genes in her than she had ever realised? She would not let herself use the euphemism 'making love', for she was still hard pressed to explain exactly how she had ended up on that bed with Angelo, engaging in the intimacies she had avoided sharing with other men. While she had always experienced a strong buzz of attraction in Angelo's radius, it had never occurred to her that it might have the power to get so out of hand. Evidently all it had taken was for her emotions to get equally out of kilter for the proverbial weak moment to have made nonsense of her moral outlook on life.

She had dropped her guard while she had sought forgetfulness from the unhappy present. Even worse, she had become intimate with a man she didn't even like, a man who had always held her at arm's length and treated her with cool indifference. No matter how she looked at what had happened she felt that she had let herself down badly and could not imagine ever meeting Angelo van Zaal again without suffering severe embarrassment.

Clutching a laden bag of keepsakes, she climbed on board a tram and found a seat. The busy streets whirred past while she tried not to think about how different Angelo had seemed once he brought the barriers crashing down by kissing her. So open, so apparently honest. *So, you're really beautiful, are you?* an unimpressed little voice jeered in her head and she went pink and laced her fingers defensively together. It would be much wiser just to put all those inappropriate memories in a mental box and put them firmly away, she decided with a hearty sense of relief at having seen that obvious solution to her mental discomfiture.

How great a risk was there, though, that she might fall pregnant? Flora did the little sums with the menstrual dates that she had refused to share with Angelo and suppressed a troubled sigh of concern, for there was no comfort to be found in those figures. Their accident, if accident it could be called, had occurred squarely in the middle of her most fertile phase. She could only pray that she would not conceive, although even that thought felt strange to a woman already engaged in an application to adopt her baby niece.

But what were her chances of success on that score? Her reddened mouth curved down. She had embarked on her adoption plans with high hopes, secure in the knowledge that she was Mariska's only surviving relative and ignorant of the fact that Angelo might also cherish a desire to adopt Willem and Julie's daughter. And Angelo, she reckoned unhappily, was going to be much stiffer competition in the adoption stakes than she had ever dreamt, because he had been engaged in looking out for Mariska ever since she was born and had already established a record of consistent care where the little girl was concerned. Nobody seemed the least bit worried that he was an unmarried single man, which she supposed was only fair considering that she was an unmarried single woman with only her time as a qualified childminder to back her application.

Furthermore it would take months for her adoption application to be properly checked out and considered and, in the meantime, Angelo had custody of her niece. Mariska would naturally become more settled in his home and more attached to him. Flora did not think her chances of winning custody of the tot from Angelo were good and the acknowledgement filled her with deep sadness. Unaware of Angelo's claim previously, she had naively believed that there would be no barrier to her

bringing little Mariska straight back home to Charlbury
St Helens with her.

Mariska greeted her aunt with smiles and chuckles
and lifted her mood. What remained of the afternoon
passed away and Anke suggested that Flora join them
for their evening meal and remain until the little girl's
bedtime. Once she realised that she would not be eating
with Angelo as well, Flora was grateful for the invitation
to extend her stay. They had a light meal in the nursery
and Flora had a lot of fun helping to bath her niece
and prepare her for bed. At one stage as she towelled
Mariska dry and the little girl succumbed to helpless
giggles she looked down into her little face and saw her
sister's delicate blonde, blue-eyed prettiness replicated
there. For an instant her eyes filled with tears again and
as she carefully got her emotions back under control she
finally appreciated how terribly tired she was. Once the
little girl was tucked up in her cot, Flora put her coat on
and headed for the stairs.

'Good evening, Flora. I didn't realise that you were
still in the house,' Angelo imparted, emerging from a
door off the imposing landing and taking her uncomfortably by surprise. Garbed in an elegant dinner jacket,
black hair spiky and damp above his lean, darkly handsome face, he looked stunningly handsome and well
groomed.

Hugely disturbed by the unexpected encounter,
Flora met his brilliant blue dark-lashed eyes and felt as
though she had fallen on an electric fence to be fried.
Disquiet ricocheted through her slim length, her cheeks
hollowing, her soft full lips compressing with tension.
'I'm afraid I stayed as long as I could with Mariska

because I'm leaving tomorrow, but now I'm absolutely bushed.'

'My driver will take you back to your hotel,' Angelo cut in smoothly.

'But I don't need…'

'I *insist*,' Angelo incised without hesitation. 'You look exhausted.'

Flora was not best pleased to be told that she looked less than her best. It did not have quite the same flattering ring as the 'beautiful' compliment had had, she reflected wryly. Nor did she like Angelo insisting anything in that dominant tone of voice that seemed to come so naturally to him. But as she parted her lips to argue the point, she belatedly realised that they were not alone.

A platinum-blonde dark-eyed woman in a very smart sleeveless white cocktail frock with a glittering diamond pendant at her throat was standing in the hall and clearly waiting on Angelo. He introduced Flora to the other woman with effortless courtesy, and Flora wondered what it would actually take to embarrass him for as far as she could see he was not even slightly ruffled by the need to make that introduction. Was Bregitta Etten his current girlfriend? When Angelo had slept with Flora earlier that day had he been unfaithful to this other woman? Or was Bregitta merely one of the endless parade of eager females in Angelo's life whom Julie had scornfully mentioned? Her sister had made it clear that Angelo was an unabashed womaniser who made the most of his freedom and Flora could only wish now that she had paid more heed to the warning and learned to be more cautious around him.

While Angelo organised Flora's lift back to the hotel,

the very beautiful blonde rested possessive stroking fingers on his arm. Flora discovered that she would very much have liked to slap that hand away from him and was horribly shocked by that instant in which she reacted like a jealous cat who wanted to scratch. Frozen several feet away from the couple, she avoided making eye contact and left the house at speed when a sleek four-wheel-drive car drew up at the front steps and the driver climbed out to open the passenger door.

'I'll phone you,' Angelo informed her calmly.

Flora turned mutinous eyes to his lean strong face and the challenge she saw there, but she was all too conscious of Bregitta's curious gaze and she forced a casual smile and a nod before climbing into the waiting car…

CHAPTER FOUR

FLORA arrived home the following afternoon and barely paused for breath before she headed round to Charlbury St Helens' veterinary surgery, which also accommodated a small boarding kennels, to pick up her pets.

Jess Martin, the youngest and newest vet to join the practice, who also lived on the premises, greeted her in the reception area. A small curvaceous brunette, Jess organised Flora's bill while the nurse went to fetch the animals from the kennels at the back. Skipper, a tiny black and white Jack Russell with more personality than size, raced out, his lead trailing, and hurled his stocky little body frantically at Flora's legs. Mango the cat, a magnificent black tom of imposing size, was in his box and steadfastly ignoring his mistress. He always sulked when she returned after leaving him.

'All present and correct,' Jess remarked, and then with a concerned look in her unusually light grey eyes, for she knew why Flora had had to board her pets at such short notice, she added, 'How are you? How was it over there?'

Flora grimaced and for a moment in receipt of that sympathetic look she did not trust herself to speak. 'I managed.'

'And your niece?' Jess asked eagerly. 'Have you got her out in the car?'

'I'm afraid it's not going to be that simple. There are quite a few legal formalities to be got through first,' Flora confided ruefully. '*And* Willem's brother, Angelo, has custody of Mariska at the minute and he's applying to adopt her as well…'

Jess looked surprised. 'But isn't he single?'

'So am I,' Flora pointed out wryly. 'And he's had a lot more contact with my niece than I've had.'

'But you'd make a terrific mother.' Jess chose to concentrate on the most positive angle. 'I've been told you were sadly missed locally when you stopped child-minding and went into the bed-and-breakfast business instead.'

Her detached house, which Flora had inherited from the great-aunt she had been named after, was set back well from the road and was sheltered from the pretty village green by mature trees. Tourists loved the village of Charlbury St Helens and Flora's guest-house business kept her very busy indeed. When her rooms were fully booked she often employed Jess Martin's mother, Sharon, to help her out. As Skipper raced down the back garden to acquaint himself with all his favourite places and Mango the cat stalked out to settle on the patio to sunbathe, Flora tried not to think about whether or not she was ever going to get the chance to bring Mariska home to England with her.

And what if you have fallen pregnant? an anxious little voice whispered at the back of her mind and all the worry that she had tried to suppress shot through her taut length like a gunshot piercing tender flesh. It would be ten days at least before she would know either way, so there was no point working herself up into a state over the issue, she told herself firmly. But Flora was still so angry with herself about what had happened in Amsterdam that she was unable to shake free of her inner turmoil.

Once she had believed that sex should be very much part of love and that it should never be separate from it; that conviction had happily guided her through the five years she had spent dating Peter, whom she had met at university and planned to marry. When Peter had dumped her after the employment tribunal, without ever having slept with her, everything that Flora had once believed in had begun to fall apart. She had wanted to believe that she and Peter were the perfect couple but had learnt the hard way that they were not. Over time, his indisputable lack of sexual interest had battered her self-esteem almost beyond hope of recall and she had switched off as far as men were concerned, too scared of being hurt and humiliated again to take a second chance on finding love.

But, in many ways, Flora had been scarred almost as much by her own childhood as by Peter, for she had never been able to forget her mother's heartbreak or her father's constant self-serving lies and deceptions. Love had almost destroyed her mother, who had suffered several episodes of serious depression before she could finally work up the strength to build a new life without her unfaithful husband. And sadly, Flora recalled wistfully, her loving mother had only lived eighteen short months after embarking on that valiant fresh start.

Yet her mother had never stopped believing in true

love and commitment. So, *how*, Flora asked herself painfully, could she have contrived to have lost her virginity to Angelo van Zaal? He hadn't even realised he was her first lover either. She had nothing in common with him. He was a man who had yet to take any woman seriously and he had offered her no promises or reassurances. Yet neither of those very sensible points had mattered once he kissed her. His kisses had burned through her like a forest fire, reducing her long-cherished convictions to ashes.

She had reached the mature age of twenty-six without realising just how vulnerable she might be with the wrong man. And Angelo was decidedly the wrong man. He was a very wealthy and sophisticated tycoon and at heart he was as cold as ice. But if that was true why was he offering to give Willem's daughter a home? Mariska was not even related to him by blood, Flora conceded ruefully, torn in opposing directions and disturbed by the bits that didn't add up in her view of him. To be fair to him he had looked out for the little girl's interests from birth. Seemingly he had also done his utmost to help Willem and Julie. Evidently Angelo had a strong streak of family loyalty and an active social conscience but neither trait made her feel any more comfortable about having shared the greatest act of intimacy there was with him.

Four days later, Angelo phoned Flora.

'Why are you calling?' she demanded sharply.

'You're phoning my house daily but contriving not to speak to me,' Angelo returned in a mocking reminder.

Flora went pink because when she rang Amsterdam

she always asked to speak to Anke. 'I didn't think you'd want to be personally involved in giving me regular bulletins on Mariska.'

'Are you always this prickly with men?' Angelo drawled silkily.

'I'm *not* prickly!' Flora snapped, her knuckles showing white as she gripped the phone tight with angry fingers, her stretched-tight control snapping at that fire-raising crack. Even his intonation set her teeth on edge. 'I assume you're calling to ask if I have any news yet on the pregnancy front and the answer is, sorry, no. I'll have a better idea by the end of next week.'

'So, we're only allowed to talk if there's bad news?'

At her end of the phone, Flora pulled a face. 'You said it—'

'For the benefit of your niece in the future, it would be sensible for us to establish a cordial relationship.'

Flora stiffened and reddened as if he had slapped her on the wrist for bad behaviour. Her teeth gritted because it was far from being the first time that Angelo van Zaal had managed to make her feel like a disruptive and rude child. Nor did she relish the obvious fact that Angelo remained confident that he would win the adoption competition. 'You should have thought of that in Amsterdam and kept your hands off me!' she snapped before she could think better of being that honest with him.

'Pot…kettle…black,' Angelo pronounced, deadpan.

And Flora was downright amazed that the violent jolt of rage that rocked her at that ruthless retaliation didn't send her screaming into orbit. A lengthy silence stretched at her end of the line as she struggled with her temper. 'I don't think we have anything more to say to each other right now,' she breathed shakily, before she set the phone down hastily lest she forget herself entirely and screech back at him like a virago.

Please, please, *please* don't let me be pregnant by him, she prayed in a frantic, feverish surge. Although at least he had been frank enough to admit that such an announcement would be 'bad news'. Yet that fact ironically only made Flora's heart sink, for she knew that if she conceived he would be anything but pleased and in even thinking that thought she felt that she was being unfair to him. After all, what rational man or woman wanted to conceive a child outside the bounds of a serious relationship? But, equally, how could she have put herself in the position of waiting to see whether or not she would fall pregnant from a casual sexual encounter? That very acknowledgement drenched her in hot shame.

Yet she could not possibly explain why her mind should immediately leap from that thought to a stirring recollection of her hands sweeping up over Angelo's muscular hair-roughened torso. Yes, he had had strong grounds for his retaliation, for she *had* found it equally impossible to keep her hands off him that afternoon.

The week that followed was very stressful for Flora. Local education colleges were staging open days and all the accommodation for miles around was filled with parents and would-be students. Flora's five rooms were fully booked and Sharon came in every day to help with the cleaning and changing of bedding as well as the breakfast rush. Every night Flora fell into bed much too tired to lie awake worrying. But when the end of the week arrived she was suddenly fiercely and anxiously aware that unusually her menstrual cycle was exhibiting definite signs of being disrupted. She wondered if stress could be making her late. The next day, she woke at noon on the decision that, without further ado, she would head for the nearest pharmacy to purchase a pregnancy test. That decided, however, she was barefoot and still in her pyjamas when her doorbell rang in a shrill burst.

Having assumed it was the lady who delivered the mail, Flora flung open the door with scant ceremony and with a piece of jam-spread toast still clutched in one hand. She was aghast to see Angelo and stared at him much as she might have stared at an alien had he dropped out of the sky onto her doorstep.

Angelo studied her with narrowed shimmering blue eyes. The faded blue cotton pyjamas and bare feet made her look very young and, taken by surprise, her eyes shone green as precious jade against her rosy complexion.

'What on earth are you doing here?' Flora questioned in a rush of dismay. 'Oh, my goodness, Mariska is all right, isn't she?'

'Mariska is fine,' Angelo murmured quietly. 'I'm more concerned right now about you.'

'I'm concerned about me too…but you didn't need to come all the way from the Netherlands to check up on me,' Flora assured him in a surge of disbelief.

'I was already coming to the UK on business. I had a meeting in London early this morning,' Angelo responded deflatingly. 'Are you planning to invite me into your home?'

Flora hesitated, reluctant to bring him into her private space, much preferring to keep him outside.

Angelo dealt her a shrewd appraisal and murmured with silken derision, 'What age are you? Twenty-six years old, or sixteen?'

'Is it my fault that you get on my nerves? I mean, at the very least you might have warned me that you were planning to visit!' Flora complained heatedly, making no attempt to hide her resentment as she stepped back reluctantly to allow him into the hall.

A little black and white terrier barked frantically at Angelo from a doorway. He wasn't accustomed to indoor animals in any of his phenomenally clean and smoothly run homes, so he ignored it. Even though the dog made an attempt to nip at his trouser legs, Flora patted it soothingly and rewarded the little animal with the toast in her hand. While idly wondering if a successful bite that drew blood would have won a second piece of toast and an all-out hug, Angelo frowned until he noted the way her clingy top rose to expose the smooth white skin of her hip and the curve of her bottom when she bent down. He had a sudden startling recollection of her pale slender body spread across that mattress on the houseboat and his big hands clenched in defiance of that image as he fought off the insidious arousal tugging at him.

'Would you like coffee?' Flora enquired, striving to employ the good manners she had been raised with.

'We haven't got time for that. You need to get dressed…and quickly,' Angelo asserted, shrugging back his cuff to check the slim gold watch on his wrist.

Flora frowned, alarmingly conscious of the manner

in which his beautiful sapphire-blue eyes lingered on her and of the lack of clothing she wore. She had never met any other man with such a powerfully sexual aura and she seriously hoped that she never did again. 'What the heck are you talking about? We haven't got time for... *what*?'

'A conversation or an argument,' Angelo responded drily. 'I've made an appointment for you with a London obstetrician and getting there on time will be a challenge.'

Her wide green eyes rounded in sheer disbelief. 'You've done *what*?' she gasped. 'Made an appointment for *me* with an *obstetrician*?'

'I'm done with hanging around waiting to find out whether or not you're pregnant,' Angelo spelt out with forthright cool, his stubborn jaw line squaring in emphasis. 'I'm assured that testing can safely be done at the earliest stage.'

Flora's lower lip had parted company from her upper because she was still shell shocked by his announcement. 'I can't believe you've got the nerve to do this to me!'

'*Por Dios,* I was waiting for you to take care of the issue and so far you haven't. Clearly it was time for me to step in.'

'No, it wasn't, you interfering...louse!' Flora clenched her teeth and swallowed a worse word while her eyes glowed with angry condemnation. 'For your information, I was planning to go out and buy a pregnancy test today...'

'I would prefer medical personnel to carry out the testing. There'll be a smaller margin for error,' Angelo pronounced stonily, standing his ground, black-lashed stunning blue eyes bright with challenge. 'If you've conceived, the sooner we know it, the better.'

Colour had already suffused Flora's cheeks. 'I'm not volunteering to be examined by some strange medic.'

'Natalie is an excellent doctor and she will be discreet. We need to know where we stand without any further delay.'

'How *dare* you meddle in my life like this?' Flora launched at him fierily and she stalked past him to take the stairs two at a time. 'I really can't stand you, Angelo!'

'But you still wouldn't kick me out of bed, *enamorada mia*,' Angelo murmured silkily.

Flora spun back to look at him, outrage roaring through her while on another level she wondered what those Spanish words meant.

'The truth hurts, doesn't it?' Angelo breathed with raw-edged confidence, reading her resentful expression with alarming accuracy. 'It's good to know that I'm not the only one suffering.'

Flora stiffened and veiled her gaze in a defensive move, but it was too late for self-protection because his lean bronzed features were already etched in her mind's eye to ensure that every inch of her was insanely aware of him. Whether waking or sleeping, she saw Angelo van Zaal in her dreams. And it seemed that even when they were arguing the hunger he could invoke stayed in the ascendant, for her breasts were swelling, the tender nipples tightening while the heat of sexual response was simmering low in her pelvis.

'We need to know what we're dealing with,' Angelo reasoned with scantily suppressed impatience.

'But this is my body,' Flora pointed out.

'I would very much appreciate it if you would consent to see the doctor today,' Angelo intoned between audibly gritted teeth.

'You are so unspeakably bossy!' Flora complained as she turned on her heel to complete her passage upstairs to her bedroom. She was furious that she was too sensible to refuse to attend the appointment just to make a point.

Angelo stepped back into the living room and realised that what he had taken for a giant furry and rather messy cushion was an obese black cat. The animal got up to prowl round his feet and then nudged up against him in a clumsy bid for attention. Already ill at ease in a cramped room overfilled with furniture and now under assault from the suddenly excessively affectionate cat, Angelo swore impatiently under his breath. The undersized dog was growling and baring its teeth at him from below the coffee table. Not a heroic beast, it was carefully maintaining cover and a safe distance from him.

Why did Flora Bennett have to argue with everything he did and said? She was intelligent enough to know that his having organised that appointment for her made sound sense, but still she would insist on forcing a confrontation over it. As for him being bossy? His lean, strong face hardened, his wide, sensual mouth twisting. It was his nature to take charge, and a wise move when he was very often the most intelligent and decisive individual in the vicinity. Naturally he needed to know whether or not she had conceived his child.

And if she had? That was one question that Angelo refused to tackle in advance. After all, she was not at all the sort of woman whom he would have chosen to bring his first child into the world. No, she was very far from being the *right* sort, he reflected grimly, his lean, darkly handsome face settling into forbidding lines of censure. Having had a sleazy affair with her married boss three years ago, Flora Bennett had then proceeded to try and blackmail her lover into giving her an undeserved financial bonus. No revelation in her history could have filled Angelo with greater contempt, for he too had been targeted in the office by ambitious female employees keen to advance their careers by offering him sexual favours. In his experience it was clever women like Flora who were often the most calculating and greedy as well as being the most dangerous.

Flora got dressed in a hurry. She picked out a simple denim miniskirt to wear with a striped top and a cotton cardigan and slid her feet into high-heeled sandals. She ran a brush through her hair to fluff it up and steadfastly ignored Angelo's shout up the stairs while she utilised her brown eyeliner and mascara and skimmed a sultry cherry colour over her lips.

'I'm on my way!' she yelled, speeding down the stairs.

Fuming at the amount of time she had wasted, Angelo paced in the hall and then, hearing her descent, swung fluidly round, only to tense at the sight of those endless long legs and slender thighs. 'That's a very short skirt,' he heard himself remark stiffly.

'No, it's not. I don't wear *very* short skirts—I just happen to have *very* long legs!' Flora snapped defensively.

Angelo found that unnecessary information, for he was already imagining those limbs wrapped round his waist again and his all-too-male body was reacting accordingly. So hard and full of repressed lust that he physically hurt, he swallowed back a curse and yanked open the front door. 'Come on,' he urged curtly.

Flora was taken aback to find a chauffeur-driven limo awaiting them on the street. She climbed into the very spacious interior and watched without surprise as Angelo flipped out a laptop to work on and proceeded to ignore her. Telling herself that she was relieved by his businesslike attitude, she lifted the English newspaper lying on the seat and proceeded to read it. As she read Angelo proved what a dynamo of business energy he was while he made and received calls in more than one language and rapped out commands and advice to various underlings. Listening to the level of innate authority and conviction with which he spoke, Flora was not at all surprised that she was seated in his limo speeding towards an appointment that he had arranged for her. It would take a very tough and obstinate woman to stand up to a male as determined as Angelo van Zaal, but she was convinced that she had the backbone if he pushed her hard enough.

It was late afternoon by the time they arrived at Dr Natalie Ellwood's smart private surgery in an upmarket part of central London. Flora sat edgily in the waiting room while Angelo continued to do business, just as he had during the journey. If someone had warned her that there was about to be a flood she would have left him to drown with his mobile phone still clutched in his hand. She had met some obsessively hard workers in her time, but Angelo van Zaal was in a class of his own. Mariska's would-be adoptive father was an unashamed workaholic.

'Angelo!' An elegant brunette in a beautifully cut trouser suit emerged wreathed in smiles and swam up to Angelo to kiss him effusively on both cheeks.

'Flora. This is Dr Ellwood. Natalie, your new patient,' Angelo drawled smoothly.

'Have you known Angelo for long?' Natalie asked Flora as she showed her into her surgery.

'No, not for long. You?' Flora could not resist asking, although she had noticed that the brunette wore a wedding ring.

'Oh, for ever. We went to university together. He's one of my oldest friends,' Natalie carolled with enthusiasm, her brown eyes resting on Flora with a bright questioning curiosity that she couldn't hide.

During the period that followed, Flora was examined and subjected to several tests. Natalie and her nurse were very pleasant. Finally, Flora sat down to face the doctor across her desk. 'Well?' she pressed nervously.

'Yes, I can confirm that you are pregnant.'

Flora lost colour. 'Are you absolutely certain?'

'Yes, I am. Is this an unintentional conception?' the brunette doctor asked delicately.

Flora was too much in shock to do anything other than nod like a rather vacant puppet. *Pregnant!* And by Angelo van Zaal! Dry-mouthed and on wobbly legs, she indicated that she did not wish to discuss the matter further and she returned to the waiting area where Angelo was engaged on yet another phone call, this time in French. Snatches of dialogue about defective materials and an inefficient supplier buzzed in and out of her head while her dazed green gaze sought out his. She encountered brilliant blue eyes of cool enquiry and stared at him with some of the shocked disbelief she was experiencing. She registered the exact moment that he realised what news she had just received because he said something curiously indistinct for a change and, lowering his phone and ending the call, he sprang restively upright.

Every time they met she forgot how tall Angelo was until he stood beside her and she was forced to look up at him, a necessity that rarely came her way, particularly not when she was sporting high heels. For a split second her mind wandered and she recalled how Peter, who had been the same height as her, had hated her to wear heels and stand taller than him.

'You're so tall for a woman,' his mother had once remarked with a raised brow, as if a woman being so tall was somehow in the poorest possible taste.

But then so many men preferred their women to be petite and delicate in stature, Flora reflected helplessly, thinking of how popular her sister, Julie, and her friend, Jemima, had invariably been with men. Being little was generally seen as cute and appealing. Being tall was somehow viewed as being less feminine and desirable.

'Let's go,' Angelo urged, his hand curving to Flora's

rigid spine. His beautiful sapphire-blue eyes had a stunned quality before he lowered his ridiculously lush black lashes to conceal his expression.

'So you're not quite as lucky as you think you are and, apparently, neither of us is infertile,' Flora remarked drolly on the way out onto the street.

'We'll discuss this in private,' Angelo pronounced crushingly.

'It's all right to be shocked,' Flora told him helplessly. 'I'm shocked as well.'

But unlike Flora, Angelo wasn't used to being shocked or put into a situation in which he was not in control of events. Suddenly, he appreciated, his life was yoked to Flora Bennett's whether he liked it or not. That was, assuming she planned to *have* his child. He swallowed back his questions and chose silence while he marshalled his thoughts.

In a world of her own, Flora sat in the limousine, struggling to adjust to the startling concept that in nine months' time she would become a mother. Her brain reminded her that there were other options that ranged from adoption to termination. The prospect of having to make either tough choice filled Flora with instinctive recoil. Eighteen months earlier, her sister had refused to consider any option other than giving birth to and keeping her child. But then Julie had been in love with Willem and he had been very much involved in that decision.

Yet Flora even now felt able to reflect that her own baby was already a part of her and, like little Mariska, would be her only other relative and the promising start to a new family circle. The very word 'family' warmed the chill of shock that still held Flora taut.

All right, admittedly, the baby wasn't planned, but life was all about rolling with the punches, wasn't it? And just as she was prepared to reorganise her life to become Mariska's mother she could hardly consider doing less when it came to her own child's future. She had money in the bank, a comfortable home and a viable business. Those acknowledgements gradually sent greater calm spilling through Flora, a calm that soothed her ragged nerves and fears while she reasoned that she could have found herself pregnant in a much worse situation.

Essentially it didn't matter how Angelo felt about her being pregnant with his child, she ruminated, and having recognised that truth it was as though a heavy weight fell from her shoulders. She sat a little straighter in her seat and felt a good deal less awkward. She was convinced that she didn't need Angelo for support and that belief acted like a shot of reassurance in her veins, for not needing a man for *anything* was a cause that lay very close to Flora's securely guarded heart…

CHAPTER FIVE

'WHERE are we?' Flora asked in dismay, lashes fluttering in bemusement as she appreciated that—unbelievably—she had actually followed Angelo blindly out of his limo into a building and, from there, into a lift.

'On the way up to my apartment. We have to talk,' Angelo informed her, his wide sensual mouth set in a deadly serious line.

At that point, Flora discovered that she had a deeply inappropriate desire to giggle. Angelo was poker-faced, the smooth, darkly handsome planes of his lean visage taut with self-discipline. He was determined not to put any real emotion on show, she realised with regret. Yet he was pure volatile male below that cool, calculated front that he showed to the world, she reasoned ruefully. She could not resist recalling the shockingly hot and explosive surge of the passion he had unleashed in Amsterdam. Heat slowly crept up from low in her tummy to the responsive peaks of her breasts, stiffening her nipples into tight dagger points below her clothing.

'Don't look at me like that, *enamorada mia*,' Angelo purred, his rich drawl low and rough-edged in pitch while he surveyed her with his amazing royal-blue eyes, the dark pupils as dilated as no doubt her own were.

Suddenly the atmosphere was thick as wet cement and the breath rattled in her throat. 'What does *enamor*—whatever—mean?'

'My lover,' Angelo supplied huskily.

'No, I'm not, not really,' she reasoned jerkily, fighting the compulsive pull of his charismatic masculinity with all her might, for every skin cell and nerve-ending she possessed was urging her to walk right into his arms.

His stunning eyes, accentuated by the ebony luxuriance of his lashes, narrowed to become even more devouring and magnetic. 'Then, what are you?'

Denying her vulnerability, Flora deliberately dropped her attention to study the floor at their feet. 'A mistake?'

'That is not how this feels,' Angelo growled, reaching out a hand to close long brown fingers round her wrist and tug her closer. But he knew he was lying, because that same word was flashing on and off like a warning neon sign at the back of his brain. Yet, as his attention slid from the pouting cherry-tinted invitation of her luscious mouth to the telling indentation of her prominent nipples below her top he had never been further from intellectual control; he was hard and erect and hungry for the tight sheath of her body and that was all that mattered to him.

As Angelo drew her to him dismay sent Flora's lashes skyward, green eyes flaring bright as jewels as she looked up at his bronzed sculpted features, scanning the slash of his high cheekbones, the jut of his arrogant masculine nose and his obstinate jaw line. This late in the day his golden-toned skin was steadily darkening with a shadow of stubble that simply highlighted his beautifully shaped mouth. Colliding with his startlingly blue eyes, she was utterly transfixed: he truly was gorgeous.

'Mistake,' she told him again unevenly. 'We're a mistake—'

Her voice died beneath the passionate onslaught of his sensual lips plunging down on hers and it was as if cautionary buzzers went off throughout her taut, quivering body. She craved him like a woman starved of oxygen, stretching up to kiss him back with fervour, needing and revelling in that heady taste of him with every fibre of her being.

She heard the whirr as the doors opened and he backed her out of the lift without breaking their connection. She stumbled in her heels until her spine was braced against a solid wall and she felt his hands splay to her hips, tilting her pelvis into provocative collision with the urgent thrust of his erection. A split second later, she was free again and reeling dizzily back against the wall for support with her body still greedily humming while she struggled to rescue her wits.

A mere step away, expelling his breath in an audible roughened hiss, Angelo thrust wide the door of his apartment for her entry. It was an effort for him to be that controlled. In fact it was a wonder that he wasn't still trying to take Flora out on the landing, he acknowledged with derision, resenting and distrusting her sexual power over him. She roused the hot-headed all-consuming sexuality he had believed he had left behind him. With Flora sex was elemental and as fierce and basic in its energy as a hurricane. Still hugely aroused, he was fighting a driving instinct to haul her back into his arms and carry her off to his bed. As a cascade of erotic imagery engulfed the imagination he had not known he had he almost groaned out loud in frustration. She was pregnant, she was carrying his child, he reminded himself doggedly. Rampant sex would only cloud that serious issue and add to the complexities of their dealings.

Flora could not look at Angelo as she preceded him into a very large modern reception room with a polished floor, sleek contemporary furniture and a wall of full height windows that offered breathtaking views of the river Thames. A deep inner trembling was still afflicting her and she was uncomfortably aware of the damp ache between her thighs and the stinging tightness of her nipples. When he touched her he turned her inside out and she hated it, for her earlier sense of keeping herself together was now entirely destroyed.

Angelo focused on her slender, graceful figure, noticing how the silky strands of her copper hair shone in the sunshine. Renewed desire pierced his tough hide like the point of a dagger sliding between his ribs. 'Obviously you'll come back to Amsterdam with me,' he heard himself say before he even knew he was going to say it, which was for him a most unnerving experience.

Wide-eyed, Flora spun back to look at his lean strong face, which, at every viewing, wreaked such havoc with her thoughts. 'Why on earth would I do that?'

'Primarily because you'll need my support now that you're pregnant.'

'I don't see why—I'm pregnant and healthy, not suf-

fering from some dreadful disease,' Flora pointed out
tartly.

Angelo rested piercing blue eyes on her. 'Are you
planning to have this baby? Or is it too soon for me to
ask you that question?'

Flora had frozen, her facial muscles pulling tight as
she wondered if he was harbouring hopes that she might
ultimately choose not to go through with the pregnancy.
She lifted her chin. 'I already know what I want to do
and I intend to have my baby,' she told him squarely.

Just as quickly Angelo was marvelling that he had
ever cherished the smallest doubt on that score. Having
a baby with a rich father was a lucrative passport to a
more comfortable lifestyle for a scheming woman. And
from the instant he had read Flora's history in that private detective's report two years earlier he had known
how ambitious and grasping she really was. But he had
chosen to take a risk without contraception and he could
only blame himself for giving her the opportunity to
hold him to ransom with a child for at least the next two
decades.

His handsome mouth forming a cynical line, he
said flatly, 'Naturally, I will support you in that decision in every way possible. But it would be easier for
me to follow through on that promise if you moved to
Amsterdam.'

'I don't need your support,' Flora proclaimed with
pride.

'You're not thinking of the wider issues at stake here,'
Angelo told her coolly. 'Mariska is in Amsterdam as
well.'

Flora stilled, because in the first fine flush of

discovering that she was pregnant she had indeed over-looked that connection and all its possibilities. 'You mean…we could share her care between us?'

'What other course would make sense now that you're also carrying my baby?' Angelo murmured drily. 'We could raise both children together.'

'Are you suggesting that we live together as well?' Flora pressed uncomfortably, colour flaring over her cheekbones as she had not grasped that more intimate aspect of his suggestion when he first mentioned the idea of her moving to the city where he lived.

'It would be the easiest solution,' Angelo pointed out with a profound lack of emotion that struck her as very nearly an insult. 'And the simplest solution is usually the best.'

In similar circumstances, Willem had once asked Julie to marry him. No, Flora had not expected Angelo to bite down on that sacrificial bullet, but the prospect of living under his roof and being forced to depend on him for all her needs filled her with consternation. In such a set-up she would lose her independence and become horribly reliant on her relationship with him working out. But if, in return, she would gain the much-desired right to be Mariska's mother…?

'Yes, I can see that my living in Amsterdam would have definite benefits from the children's point of view,' Flora conceded grudgingly. 'I would certainly like to be able to see Mariska every day and be a real part of her life rather than an occasional visitor—'

'But?' Angelo cut in, impatient for the objection he sensed coming and frustrated by her inexplicable reluc-tance to embrace the rich and privileged lifestyle that he had just offered her. He wondered if he needed to spell out the material advantages with greater clarity.

'I'm very independent. I like my own corner, my own way of life.'

'Yet you insist that you want to adopt Mariska.'

'I do, but you're not being frank enough to tell me what I need to know,' Flora condemned, lifting her bright head high with a glint of challenge in her clear green eyes. 'Exactly what kind of relationship are you offering me? Do you expect me to be a parenting partner and friend?'

'A lover.' That very frank contradiction slammed back at Flora like a crack of thunder, although he had not raised his voice in the slightest.

Flora was shaken. 'A l-lover?' she stammered uncertainly, taken aback by an angle she had not foreseen. 'I assumed you were talking about us coming to some platonic arrangement.'

Angelo's brilliant gaze was hot electric blue as amusement and sexual heat combined in his compelling appraisal, while a wolfish smile tugged at the corners of his handsome mouth. 'I don't think that platonic would work very well for us. I am very powerfully attracted to you, *enamorada mia*.'

The unashamed fire in that steady look sent wicked heat and anticipation hurtling straight to the most sensitive places on Flora's body. Uneasy at that rush of physical response and bemused by his bold statement of desire, Flora shifted position, her face burning pink as she struggled to think clearly. 'So, you're actually proposing that we live together in a relationship that would go much further than simply making a home for Mariska and the baby I'm expecting?'

This time it was Angelo who stilled to shoot her a questioning narrowed glance, his lean, darkly handsome features annoyingly unforthcoming. 'How much further?'

Flora recognised his tension and wariness. 'Have you really thought this proposition through, Angelo?'

'If I had not, I would scarcely have suggested it,' he fielded with cutting assurance.

But Flora was not easily cut off in full flow and an intense need to know exactly what he was offering her was now driving her. 'But you're being much too casual for something so serious,' she objected with a toss of her head, copper-coloured hair dancing back from her cheekbones. 'You're asking me to move in with you and I'm asking you on what terms would I be living with you?'

An ebony brow elevated, his stubborn jaw line clenching hard, his tone clipped and discouraging. 'Terms?'

If anything his reluctance to spell out the boundaries only made Flora more suspicious of his motives. 'Terms,' she repeated unapologetically.

'Obviously I would take care of all your expenses and you would have access to every material thing that a woman wants.'

'I can take care of my own expenses, Angelo. I don't need financial assistance and I don't need to be spoiled either. You said we would be lovers,' she reminded him uncomfortably.

Angelo shifted a broad shoulder. 'What more can you possibly want?'

Flora ground her teeth together and momentarily looked away from him, her hands clenching in aggravation. Just then, she would have loved to pour a bucket of cold water over him in punishment for his unwillingness to clarify his proposition. Did he not trust any woman or was it just her? He behaved as if words were handcuffs and chains that might come back to imprison him. 'Most people expect certain guarantees before they give up their own home and move into someone else's—particularly when there are children involved. Upheaval is very bad for children,' she spelt out loftily. 'And Mariska has already suffered quite enough change in her life.'

His beautiful eyes semi-screened by luxuriant lashes, Angelo released his breath in a slow measured hiss. 'What sort of guarantees are you asking for?'

'The obvious: stop acting like you're thick as a brick!' Flora launched back at him in growing anger. 'You know what I'm asking! How committed would you be to making this relationship work?'

'I'm not into discussing the finer points of relationships,' Angelo declared, slamming yet another door closed in her face.

'So, end of that conversation. I'm not moving to Amsterdam to live with a guy who's so immature he can't even talk about what he wants and expects from me or himself!' Flora shot back at him wrathfully.

'I am not immature, merely experienced enough to know that the instant a list of rules is drawn up in an affair I will most probably feel the need to break those rules,' Angelo drawled smooth as silk.

'Well, thanks, too, for that opportune warning. I

definitely won't be moving to Amsterdam on those terms!' Flora tossed back at him in a tone sharp with scorn and antagonism that masked the painful sense of disappointment that she was experiencing. She was as hurt as she was annoyed. 'I don't think that you entertaining yourself with other women would help us to make a happy home for young children. I grew up in a divided home and I know exactly what I'm talking about, Angelo!'

'You're being unrealistic. None of us can see into the future. What guarantees can I possibly give you?' Angelo countered levelly.

'Before I abandon my home and way of life to take a chance on depending on you in another country? At the very least, your commitment to offering me an exclusive relationship. But I can see that you're unwilling to promise fidelity,' Flora contended flatly, clashing with his stunningly blue eyes without flinching, even as another sharp little pain slivered through her at that wounding knowledge. 'And I'm afraid that I won't settle for anything less.'

'Now you're being unreasonable,' Angelo breathed curtly. 'I've never given any woman such a pledge.'

Flora grimaced, for she now knew her true value in his eyes. He might want her but evidently he already knew that he didn't want her enough to make sacrifices or promises that might offer her any hope of a viable future with him. He wanted her only for the moment and he wasn't prepared to make a longer-term commitment that would reduce his sexual options. 'Which really says all I need to know about you.'

'But what about Mariska's needs? What about the

child you're carrying? Don't they deserve that we should at least *try* to live together?' Angelo demanded rawly, outraged by her inflexible outlook. He had made what he deemed to be a very generous offer. He had never asked a woman to live with him before. Nor had any woman ever boldly confronted him with an in-your-face demand for exclusivity. He had certainly been in receipt of plenty of hints and persuasive moves on that score, but he had always set a very high value on his freedom and had always moved on from one affair to the next with a light heart. But this woman was different from all her many predecessors in one crucial field, he conceded grimly. She carried his baby in her womb. But did that give her the right to hold him to ransom and make such a far-reaching demand? Most women would have been honoured to be invited to live in his home and share his bed, but she had transformed his invitation into some kind of backhanded affront. His lean, compellingly attractive features stubbornly taut, he thought she was demanding too much and he dug his heels in with every atom of his stubborn strength of will.

'I think that the children deserve something more from us than us just *trying* to live together. You would have to be more committed to the relationship than you obviously are prepared to be. I'm not interested in your money. Although I have no intention of becoming your temporary mistress, I don't think that you see me as anything more than that. Let's not discuss it any more,' Flora urged with a forced and strained smile, keen as she was to sidestep further debate on the thorny topic. 'It's not doing us any good to argue about it.'

Usually more than willing to sidestep female

aggression and disagreement, Angelo was taken aback by the furious flash of dissatisfaction and sense of injustice that gripped him when she chose to bring their dialogue to what he saw as a premature conclusion. Clearly it was a matter of her way or the highway... *How dared she* lay down the law to him in such a manner?

'How do you propose to continue your relationship with Mariska?' Angelo enquired with scantily leashed contempt.

Flora lifted her chin. 'I'll fly over and visit as often as I can.'

'It won't be an adequate substitute for you being on the spot.'

Flora lost colour, guilt and more than a touch of doubt assailing her. 'It would be much harder for Mariska if I was there for her for a few weeks and then gone again.'

Angelo dealt her a grim appraisal. 'It's not that straightforward.'

'Oh, I think it would be with a guy like you—used to having his options and enjoying them no matter what the cost,' Flora returned without hesitation, as she knew all too well that a sexually predatory man got bored with just one woman and preferred variety in the bedroom. Her father had never hesitated to indulge himself with an attractive woman and, regardless of his marriage or his children, had always put his own desires of the moment first.

Outrage at that rejoinder cut through Angelo in a boiling hot swathe, since he was neither self-indulgent nor destructive with women. Female companionship and sex were essential to him and it had never been a challenge for him to fulfil his needs with like-minded partners. It was rare for his affairs to end on a sour note because his lovers understood from the outset that he was not promising either everlasting love or fidelity. Did Flora really expect to dictate rules to him? What sort of men was she accustomed to dealing with?

'I only visit the UK about once or twice a month,' Angelo intoned curtly. 'It will be difficult for me to offer you the level of support that you deserve.'

'I'll manage just fine on my own,' Flora asserted, lifting her head high and watching anger flare in his bright blue eyes as he translated her response as yet another offensive rejection.

'I will at least accompany you to your medical appointments,' Angelo declared on a decided note of challenge.

'That's unnecessary...'

'Clearly you intend to shut me out completely!' Angelo growled in a driven undertone.

'Not at all,' Flora fielded uncomfortably. She was already moving back to the hall to take her leave, keen to evade the stab of conscience beginning to gnaw at her. After all, lots of men evaded their responsibility when a woman fell pregnant and Angelo did deserve her respect for his determination to give her his support. 'But I do think that once the baby is born we'll have more to talk about.'

Infuriated by her determination to keep him at arm's length until that stage, Angelo strode after her. 'My driver will take you home and I'll stay in touch. Please don't tell me that that's not necessary either!'

Those words literally bubbling on the tip of her ready

tongue, Flora reddened and sealed her soft lips closed again. They were at daggers drawn and she had not intended that but she did not see how she could change the situation. He had expected certain responses from her and he had lost patience with her when she failed to deliver those responses. He was a very powerful personality and he was accustomed to women falling in with his wishes. Flora, however, believed that it would be downright dangerous to get more deeply involved with Angelo van Zaal when the relationship would clearly be of short duration. The eventual breakdown of a relationship between them would only create bad feeling that might well jeopardise her ongoing ties with Mariska, as well as his with their unborn child. As someone whose own childhood had been deeply scarred by quarrelling, unhappy parents, Flora was keen not to inflict that lost sense of pain, fear and bewilderment on any other child.

Lean, dark face sardonic, Angelo felt bitter as he watched Flora leave his apartment. It was many years—indeed not since his stepmother had died—since Angelo had felt so angry with and exasperated by a woman. Once again, Flora Bennett had taken him by surprise. He had assumed she would grab at the opportunity to move in with him and not only for mercenary reasons either. The sexual heat between them was mutual and strong and in his opinion more than sufficient to sustain a relationship, yet she was refusing to take account of it. It was very hard for him to accept that although his first baby was on the way its mother wanted nothing to do with him. If that was her attitude now, how much was he likely to see of his child once it was born? His handsome mouth twisted. And all because she had deemed him unworthy for refusing to declare that there would never be another woman in his life.

Flora settled into her bed that night and fought off a powerful desire to picture what life might have been like living with Angelo in Amsterdam. It wouldn't have lasted five minutes, she told herself staunchly. She would get hurt and humiliated when he became bored with her and then sought out other females for variety. After all, she was no sex goddess and he was a very good-looking, very rich tycoon. He was the sort of guy who would always be spoilt for choice and subject to temptation when it came to women. Besides, a brief and ultimately unsuccessful live-in arrangement would only have confused and upset Mariska; the little girl deserved better from the adults she had to depend on in her life.

But what, a little voice dared to ask, if it worked out between her and Angelo? What if Angelo was prepared to agree that she would be the only woman in his life for the duration of their relationship? In the darkness, Flora's eyes shone at that unlikely but energising image of life as it might be in a perfect world. What if she was letting her fears rule her too far? What if she was wrong not to even give Angelo a chance?

At that point, Flora turned over and punched her pillow with unnecessary force. Next she would be believing that a fairy ready to grant her three wishes might be living at the foot of the garden, she scolded herself in exasperation. Angelo was not in love with her, so why would he give up other women for her benefit? He only saw her as a temporary aberration, a short-term affair, and nothing lasting was likely to come from such a weak foundation.

Her mother's experience had taught Flora the lesson that it very often was women who took the greatest responsibility for their children and made the biggest sacrifices. Her childhood had been deeply scarred by her quarrelling, ill-suited parents. Although being a single parent was not the lifestyle she had foreseen for herself, she soon convinced herself that she had made the *right* choice in opting to pretty much go it alone with her pregnancy...

CHAPTER SIX

ANGELO slid lithely out of his limousine and studied the ivy-clad prettiness of Flora's detached village home. There were three cars parked in the driveway. He frowned, wondering how many guests she had staying and how she was coping.

But then, such matters were none of his business according to Flora, he reflected with a grim light clouding his vivid blue eyes. Over the past two months it had become increasingly plain to him that Flora intended to keep him at a distance where he could neither interfere nor offer his assistance. His phone calls had met with stilted impersonal responses from her that told him virtually nothing. His attempt to pay her a monthly allowance to enable her to take life a little easier had been roundly rejected as well.

Angelo was bewildered by her attitude. Nothing about Flora Bennett added up and Angelo hated mysteries. If the private investigator's report he had received on Flora and her sister two years ago had been on target, cold hard cash should have paved an easy path to Flora's heart. She should have been eager to fit in with his plans and reap the generous rewards of pleasing him. That she was not eager or even willing told him that either the report had got her wrong or she was playing a much more clever game of deception than he had so far had cause to suspect. Yet would a materialistic woman turn down the opportunity to move in with a billionaire and live in the lap of luxury? And why would she refuse his financial help? Or was that a ruse to come back later through the offices of a court of law and sue him for a final settlement amounting to many, many thousands of pounds? That was perfectly possible, he acknowledged grimly.

His suspicions about Flora's motives did not make it any easier for him to handle the mother of his future child. Furthermore, for the first time in his adult life, Angelo was dealing with a tricky relationship with a woman instead of turning his back and walking away, deeming her too much trouble to be worthy of his time and patience. He was not enjoying the process either, for her every rebuff infuriated him.

Indeed the problems created by Flora's continuing hostility were matched by the widespread disruption of Angelo's once regimented and perfectly composed mind. Angelo was uneasy with the unfamiliar feelings of frustration and anger regularly assailing him. His concentration was no longer what it was, nor was his famously single-minded focus zeroed in on business goals alone. All of a sudden, he was suffering from moments of abstraction. He was also noticing every pregnant woman and every redhead in his vicinity. He was even more disturbed by the fact that he had not slept with a single woman since Flora. Celibacy agreed with Angelo even less than mental turmoil. Sex had always been his foolproof means of unwinding from his demanding schedule. Sex had never been any more complicated for him than a good workout at the gym. But Angelo had recently become worryingly impervious to the sexually sophisticated women who had once entertained him most effectively outside working hours. His highly active libido had taken a hike and he had no idea why or what to do about it.

He hit Flora's doorbell, knowing in advance that his uninvited visit would be as welcome as a snow shower in summer. In an unusually disorganised and last minute decision the night before, Angelo had reached the end of his patience and he had flown over to England too late at night even to call Flora. The door of her home was opened by a stranger and the hall was confusingly awash with more strangers. He counted three middle-aged couples, presumably Flora's current boarders.

'Where's Flora?' he asked.

'Upstairs in the bathroom…she's not well,' one of the women informed him. 'We're getting ready to leave.'

'*Without* our breakfast,' a disgruntled older man pronounced.

'If you'll give me a few minutes to check on Flora, I'll sort that out for you,' Angelo declared, his concern at the news that Flora was unwell prompting him to take the stairs two at a time. It took him a minute or two to establish which door led to the bathroom.

That achieved, he rapped loudly on the solid wood. 'Flora? It's Angelo. Are you all right?' he asked urgently.

Flora was very far from being all right. White and shaking, she clung to the edge of the sink to steady her wobbly lower limbs. She felt like death warmed up and her brain was woozy, thoughts coming only slowly. Why on earth had Angelo come to see her again? She felt too sick to protest as she usually would have done. Sickness had a way of making one concentrate only on the immediate. In any case, Angelo was so determined that protest would have been a waste of time and energy. Like a steamroller chugging unstoppably downhill Angelo just kept on rolling no matter what she said or did.

Flora opened the door a crack and clung to the handle for support. Angelo pressed the door wider open and she stepped back awkwardly. She was so much more colourful and somehow *real* than other women, he thought helplessly, immediately admiring the flame colour of her bright hair against her creamy skin and the sheer leggy elegance of her tall, slender figure. And his libido, which had steadfastly refused to react to a single one of the nubile models whose numbers were stored in his mobile phone, suddenly took high-voltage flight. That surge of intense sexual arousal froze Angelo in place and the source of it so much took him aback that he then viewed Flora with instantly cooler and more critical eyes. Just as quickly he saw the change in her and consternation took hold of him instead.

'I'm fine…I'm just suffering from nausea,' she told him wryly. 'Welcome to the reality of being pregnant.'

But Angelo was shocked by her shadowed eyes and pallor and he recognised from the sharpness of her cheekbones and the loose fit of her clothing that she had lost a good deal of weight since he had last seen her. '*Dios mio*, you look terrible,' he breathed, backtracking from his opinion a mere sixty seconds earlier when just a welcome glimpse of her warm familiar colouring had instantly convinced him that she looked terrific.

Pain pierced Flora as she still secretly cherished the memory of him calling her beautiful. This revised opinion hit her hard, even though she was aware that she looked less than her best in jeans and a shirt with not even a dash of make-up to brighten her up. Angelo, on the other hand, looked absolutely effortlessly gorgeous. The breeze had tousled his thick black cropped hair and scored colour along the splendid line of his high cheekbones, accentuating his superb bone structure. Even this early in the day his golden skin was beginning to shadow with dark stubble across his stubborn jaw line and round his wide sensual mouth. He was more casually dressed than she was accustomed to seeing him in jeans and a fine expensive sweater worn with a very masculine jacket. Her mouth running dry, she was quite overpowered by his magnetic presence for a couple of minutes.

'You should lie down for a while,' Angelo instructed.

'I can't,' Flora groaned. 'I have guests waiting for their breakfast downstairs…' And she was dreading the prospect, having already learned that certain cooking smells could make her feel horribly nauseous.

'I will deal with them. Go to your bed,' Angelo urged with impressive assurance.

Flora had never seen Angelo as a guy likely to be handy in the kitchen and she hovered uncertainly. '*But…*'

'Go and lie down,' he said again, stepping to one side to thrust open the door to the room he had already identified as hers.

The sight of her comfortable bed was all the pressure Flora needed at that moment and she crossed the corridor to gratefully collapse in a heap on top of the duvet. Her weary limbs were heavy as iron. She was so tired, indeed she was convinced that she had never been so tired in her whole life. The bouts of constant sickness that seized hold of her at all times of day and the exhaustion of continually feeling unwell had conquered her stubborn spirit as nothing else could have done.

Angelo closed the door on her and rang the country hotel he had checked into late the night before. Within minutes he was ushering Flora's paying guests out to his limousine and instructing his driver to take them to the hotel for their breakfast. Everybody more than happy with that new arrangement, he returned to Flora and explained what he had done.

Flora studied him with thoughtful green eyes, reluctantly impressed by his adroit handling of the situation. She would have enjoyed seeing him wielding a frying pan in her kitchen, but the shrewd organisational and negotiating skills he had just displayed were in all probability basic van Zaal business traits.

'I appreciate that I know very little about pregnant women,' Angelo said with enormous tact, keeping quiet about his current bedside reading, which would in fact have proved that he knew much more about being pregnant than Flora did. 'And naturally I've heard of morning sickness, but I really don't think it's normal for you to be feeling this ill. You should see a doctor.'

'I already have,' Flora sighed wearily, turning over and tucking her hand below her cheek as she made herself as comfortable as possible. 'My GP says that some women suffer like this and that hopefully it will slacken off soon.'

'I would still like you to agree to see Natalie again,' Angelo imparted.

Already drifting off to sleep, Flora gave him a rare nod of assent, pathetically willing to consult anyone who might have the power to make her condition a little more bearable. Right at that moment, she felt as though her pregnancy had taken over her entire life, sapping the energy and confidence that she had always taken for granted.

His big powerful frame alive with brooding tension, Angelo watched her sleep, his lean dark features set in tough lines and his jaw at an aggressive angle. He lifted a throw lying folded on a chair and shook it out to cover her up. Then he stepped out again to contact Natalie on his mobile phone and share his concerns. Nothing his friend said soothed his apprehension on Flora's behalf.

Flora wakened when Angelo touched her shoulder and gazed straight up into azure-blue eyes surrounded by swirling ebony lashes. Her heart skipped a whole beat inside her chest. 'How long have I been asleep?'

'About two hours. I'm only waking you now because Natalie wants to see you this afternoon,' he explained.

'Have I got time for a shower?' Flora sat up very slowly, too well aware that sudden movements were likely to bring on dizziness and nausea.

Freshening up with a shower lifted Flora's spirits. As she got dressed she reflected that, although she had lost weight in recent weeks, her shape had changed and not for the better. With her trousers already refusing to button at her waist, she donned recent purchases, a skirt with a partially elasticated waist and a top in a larger size than she usually wore. Even though it was early in her pregnancy, her breasts had already swelled by a couple of cup sizes and her waist seemed to be vanishing even faster. Reflecting on those unwelcome alterations to her body, Flora grimaced, deciding that what attraction she had possessed was now very much on the wane. Praying that the sickness would remain at bay, she joined Angelo in the limousine.

'Why were you trying to cater to so many people without help?' Angelo asked her then.

A few weeks earlier, Sharon Martin, Flora's part-time employee, had been diagnosed with cancer and the older woman was currently undergoing treatment. Flora had not managed to find a replacement for Sharon and, reluctant to cancel bookings at short notice, she had contrived as best she could to manage alone.

'It's been a struggle,' she admitted reluctantly.

'Yet you still found the time to spend several days in Amsterdam with Mariska,' Angelo remarked.

'She's so young. If I don't make the effort to see Mariska regularly, she'll forget who I am,' Flora pointed out ruefully.

Angelo answered a phone call and while he was talking Flora kicked off her shoes and curled up into a comfortable position, resting her cheek down on the cool leather back of the passenger seat. A blink of an eye later she was fast asleep again and he had to shake her awake at the end of their journey.

'Sorry,' Flora framed, politely shielding a yawn before finger combing her tumbled coppery hair back from her brow in some embarrassment. 'I've a lot of sleep to catch up on.'

In the waiting room she watched Angelo, only to redden uncomfortably when she realised that he was watching her. On their previous visit to Dr Ellwood's surgery, Angelo had very effectively tuned out of the proceedings and done as much business as if he were still at the office. Now his obvious disquiet touched her and stirred her conscience because she knew she had made things difficult when he had tried to stay in touch with her. If he had asked her why she would not have had a ready answer for him, because even she did not fully understand her often hostile attitude to him. What she did know was that when she focused on Angelo van Zaal's darkly handsome features she felt intensely vulnerable and scared and that was more than sufficient to ensure she stayed away from him and avoided his influence.

Natalie called Flora into her surgery and discussed her symptoms before giving her an examination and a blood test. After that the nurse showed Flora into the small room where the ultrasound scanning machine was kept and helped her get up onto the couch in readiness.

'Angelo wants to know if he can join us,' Natalie told her, popping her head round the door.

Startled by that request, Flora started to sit up. 'Er...'

But Angelo appeared in the brunette's wake, and to object struck Flora as petty, particularly when she was about to receive her very first view of the baby in whom Angelo appeared to have an equal interest. She lay back down again while Angelo stationed his tall, powerful frame in a discreet location by the wall, his keen gaze welded to the screen while Natalie talked about what they could hope to see at this stage of Flora's pregnancy.

'Ah, yes, this is what I suspected,' Natalie remarked with satisfaction as she moved the transducer over the gel slicked across Flora's stomach. 'There to the left, is the first baby…see the heartbeat…and there is the second baby…' for an instant the doctor paused and then drew in an audible breath before continuing '…and tucked in behind that one, is the *third* baby! My word, I already suspected that you might be expecting twins, but you're carrying triplets, Flora. That's probably why you've been feeling so very sick. Your hormones are in override.'

'*Triplets?*' Flora parrotted, her voice sounding as squeezed as if someone were bouncing up and down on her lungs. 'You mean that there's three of them?'

A large hand closed over her nervously clenching fingers. 'That's amazing news,' Angelo pronounced with admirable conviction.

Astonished, Flora tipped back her head to look up at him and noted that he was unusually pale. She reckoned that he too was shocked by Natalie's revelation but simply better at hiding his reactions than Flora was. Flora was stunned and totally overwhelmed by the prospect of three babies rather than one. She had naturally imagined how she might cope if she won custody of Mariska but had calculated her niece would be a toddler at a different stage of development by the time she gave birth.

The news that she was carrying triplets turned all her

careful plans for the future upside down. It would be a challenge to continue her bed-and-breakfast business and even part-time childcare costs would be *huge*. For the first few months of motherhood she would definitely have to live off the money in her bank account. On the other hand, that cash bonus was her only nest egg and with the needs of at least three children to meet in the future she realised that it would probably be wiser to try and work and save the money she currently had in the bank.

'I can't tell you the sex of the babies yet. It's too early,' Natalie Ellwood informed them cheerfully. 'Are there any multiple pregnancies in either family?'

As Flora shook her head in a negative motion Angelo opened his mouth and then closed it again, deeming what he had been about to say concerning his own early history inappropriate. He knew that a multiple pregnancy carried greater risks and it worried him that Flora was already far from well. Registering that the news about their triplets had struck her dumb, he lifted her down off the couch with care and accompanied her back into Natalie's surgery. Flora, still in complete shock from what she had learned, was urged to avoid stress, rest more and eat little and often in an effort to regain the weight she had lost. If the sickness continued at the same rate, Natalie said she would need to go into hospital to receive treatment. Flora was shaken by that last warning because it had not once occurred to her that her health and that of her unborn baby might be at risk. Unborn *babies*, her mind adjusted, while she recognised that she would need all her health and strength to carry three babies as close to term as possible.

'I would like to take you back to Amsterdam with me,' Angelo pronounced before they had even left the building. 'No, don't argue with me...think of the advantages. You can stay in bed all day if you like. You won't have to cook for yourself and everything will be done for you. You'll have Mariska to fill your days instead of demanding guests.'

'And Mariska will never ask me to cook a fried egg,' Flora mumbled, striving not to get caught up in the lazy blissful imagery of the dream world he was describing. 'I'm used to working and keeping busy, Angelo.'

'But right now you need some time out to regain your health.'

It was true; there was no arguing with that reminder. Natalie had emphasised that tiredness and stress were very probably only making the sickness Flora was suffering from worse. And she knew she had lost more weight than was good for her. She would also have Mariska to keep her occupied. At that moment, the proverbial *weak* moment, an image of the picturesque streets and canals of Amsterdam and having meals cooked for her carried considerable appeal for Flora.

Angelo tucked her into the limousine. Although he had said and done nothing to reveal the fact, the prospect of becoming the father of four children had knocked him sideways. Only three months earlier he'd had no plans to have any children of his own. But now, he gazed down at Flora and, in one of those inexplicable moments of flawed concentration that currently afflicted him, he was immediately sidetracked by the view. From that angle the newly full rounded globes of her breasts and her shadowy cleavage were visible below the modest neckline of her cotton top. There was something incredibly powerfully erotic about that illicit glimpse and he remembered the taste of her and the fresh scent of her skin. That fast lust ran through Angelo like a river of lava and the swelling hardness at his groin became a greedy ache. A muscle at the corner of his handsome mouth pulling taut, he swung in beside her.

Brilliant sapphire-blue eyes sought out hers in a sudden assault. 'I still want you in my bed, *enamorada mia.*'

In the aftermath of what they had just found out, Flora was startled by his candour. That bold husky reiteration sent tiny quivers of awareness darting through her tense body. His potent emphasis shook her as, removed from his radius, Flora had once again stopped seeing herself as a sexual being. Soft pink mouth opening, her tongue slid out to moisten her dry lower lip.

'You are *so* hot,' Angelo growled thickly, and he bent his proud dark head to crush her lips under his, his tongue delving into the moist and tender interior with a darting erotic finesse that sent the blood drumming madly through her veins and brought her hands up to clutch at his arms.

Responses that had bothered Flora in uneasy dreams that even she could not control leapt straight back to life. A squirming, curling heat shimmered low in her pelvis, dispatching tingling warmth to private places. Her nipples pinched into stiff straining crests and the tender flesh at the heart of her dampened while she held her body taut in defiance of that response.

'I want you,' Angelo husked, running his sensual mouth down her slender neck in a way that made her shiver violently, while his hand reached below her top to toy with the engorged peak of one breast.

In one urgent motion Flora jerked free and contrived to move a good two feet from him. Wide-eyed and flushed, she muttered hurriedly, 'No!'

His ebony lashes dipped low over his extraordinary jewel-bright eyes. 'I'm sorry. You excite me so much that I even contrived to forget that you aren't well.'

'That's okay,' Flora framed before she could think better of it, wanting to shut the door, as it were, but not bar and lock it for ever. Even with all her hormones leaping and bounding like spring rabbits through her rebellious body, she would not have confessed why she had drawn back from him. Being ill or unwilling had nothing to do with it. As she smoothed down her top wild horses would not have forced her to admit that she had had to put some space between them before he discovered that she was wearing an industrial-strength bra with a line of hooks and thick straps. *You excite me?* Well, he would not have retained that impression for long, she reflected with a shrinking quiver of embarrassment. At the same time she was helplessly thrilled that he still appeared to find her sexually attractive.

'Just not now,' she added, striving to add a discreet hint of encouragement for the future while her face burned hotter than a fire. 'In Amsterdam.'

'So, you'll come back with me,' Angelo breathed with intense satisfaction.

And Flora could not meet his questioning gaze, because there was something about him that made her so ridiculously impulsive and, incredibly, unbelievably, she had just agreed to move in with him without thinking it through in triplicate and over the space of at least a week of sleepless nights. And now, if she immediately took the declaration back, he would think she was a total airhead who didn't know what she was doing or saying. Dismayed by a recklessness that ran contrary to her usual nature, however, she could not withstand the urge to try and backtrack. 'My pets would have to come with me as well and I would have an enormous amount of packing to do even for a short stay.'

'I'll organise everything for you. I don't want you tiring yourself out.'

'I don't know if I can live with you…'

Long brown fingers tilted up her chin so that she collided with his cerulean-blue gaze in which ferocious determination was writ large. 'But it costs nothing to *try*…'

Flora disagreed but she kept the thought to herself. She didn't want to get used to him being around if he wasn't going to stay with her. She didn't want to fall for him. She didn't want to get hurt. She had put all her eggs in one basket with Peter and at the end of the day had turned out to be anything but his ideal woman. Would she ever be any man's ideal woman? If she had not fallen pregnant, would Angelo be inviting her to move in with him? Would she even have heard from him again? Worrying along those mortifying lines sent a cold chill through her and severely wounded her pride.

'You do way too much agonising over things,' Angelo informed her abruptly, one hand closing over hers, his vivid azure gaze narrowed and intense on her expressive face. 'We have *four* children to consider now,' he stressed. 'If you can't be optimistic, at least attempt to be practical.'

His advice engulfed her like a landslide and was even less welcome. Practical was a very dirty word to Flora at that instant. She did not want Angelo van Zaal to settle for her because she was carrying his triplets and also happened to be Mariska's aunt. She needed more; she desperately longed to be wanted for herself.

'I don't want to be practical…I want to be loved,' Flora admitted gruffly before she could lose her nerve and duck making that very personal admission.

Angelo gave her a look of complete exasperation as if she had suggested something utterly outrageous. 'I've never been in love in my life!'

It was Flora's turn to raise her brows. *'Never?'* she pressed in disbelief.

'Not since I succumbed to an infatuation as a teenager,' Angelo derided, his wide sensual mouth curling.

It was depressing news but it also gave Flora a very strong desire to slap him. 'I suppose you don't believe in love?'

'I believe in lust.'

Flora flattened her lips into an unimpressed line and lifted her chin in silent challenge.

'Go on, confess,' Angelo murmured with silken scorn. 'You fell madly in love with me that day on the houseboat and that's the only reason you slept with me!'

In receipt of that sardonic crack, Flora was so desperate to slap him and working so hard to restrain that urge that she trembled. 'I'm afraid I still can't explain *why* I slept with you.'

'Lust,' Angelo told her with immense assurance.

Flora's self-control snapped clean through as if he had jumped on it. 'Well, if that's all we've got together, I'm not coming to Amsterdam. I can find lust anywhere with a one-night stand and I don't need to leave the country to do it!'

Angelo shot her a blistering look of dazzling blue fury and frustration. 'You're being totally unreasonable—I can't give you love. I can respect you, care for you, like you and lust after you, but don't make a demand I can't hope to meet!'

Respect, care, like, lust, she enumerated and her chin came up even higher. 'Why not? What's wrong with me?' she shot back at him baldly.

Her obstinacy in sticking to her point sent Angelo's temper shooting up the scale. 'Nothing is wrong with you. I just don't *do* love and romance!'

Flora lifted and dropped her slim shoulders in a shrug of finality. 'Well, I feel too young and lively to settle for respect and liking!'

Angelo ground his even white teeth together and mentally counted to ten. It didn't help him overcome the suspicion that she kept on raising the bar he had to reach to heights he had no desire to aspire to. 'No matter what I offer you, it's never enough!'

'Be warned: our differences cut both ways. I might come and live with you and then fall madly in love with some other guy,' Flora pointed out dulcetly.

'No, you won't, *enamorada mia,*' Angelo told her with ferocious cool. 'I won't give you that kind of freedom.'

Her eyes danced with provocation. 'You work long

hours. Are you planning to lock me up every night in the cellar?'

'No. I plan to keep you far too busy in bed!' Angelo ground out. 'You won't have the energy to chase other men.'

'How do I know you're not all talk and no action?' Flora tossed back before she could think better of it.

His mouth closed over hers again with passionate punitive force. He crushed her to his lean, powerful body and her every skin cell leapt with sensual energy, sensation swelling her breasts and sentencing her to a bone-deep ache between her thighs. He kissed her until she was breathless and trembling and strung high on a hunger more powerful than any she had ever known. To catch her breath she had to tear her mouth from his and she was so weak in the aftermath with the lust she had decried that she bowed her brow down on his shoulder while she fought to get a hold on herself again. He had the power to turn her inside out with a single kiss and the awareness shocked her.

'I'm just warning you,' she contrived to trade in a final assault. 'Lust isn't enough for me and if I meet someone else who—'

Angelo rested a long brown finger against her parted lips to silence her, his narrowed gaze bright and fierce. 'I will make it enough, *enamorada mia*,' he told her rawly...

CHAPTER SEVEN

LITTLE more than a week after having that conversation, Flora received a visit from her friend, Jemima, whom she had not seen for several months. Jemima was married to Alejandro, a Spanish aristocrat, with whom she had two children, Alfie and Candida. Flora had got into the habit of visiting the family at their castle in Spain until Mariska had become an orphan, from which time Flora's trips abroad had taken her to see her niece in the Netherlands instead.

Before she arrived, Jemima, a tiny beautiful blonde with big blue eyes, was already aware that Flora had fallen pregnant. Brought up to speed on the latest developments, Jemima was quick to offer her opinion. 'Of course you should move to Amsterdam and give the relationship a chance. If everything works out between you and Angelo it will be wonderful for your niece and for those babies you're carrying.'

At that advice, Flora grimaced. 'But what if it doesn't work out?'

'That's a risk you have to take. When Alejandro and I reconciled I didn't want to take that risk either,' Jemima admitted to her friend, referring to the reality that she and her husband had lived apart for a couple of years before having a second go at making their marriage work for the sake of their son, Alfie. 'You're scared of being hurt. You're afraid to let your life go here in England, but you have to take those chances before you can find out if you and Angelo are meant to be together.'

'What happened between us was just an accident,' Flora argued ruefully. 'I don't think Angelo and I *are* meant to be together.'

'Flora, you haven't trusted a man since your engagement to Peter bit the dust,' Jemima remarked ruefully.

Flora sighed. 'It's probably been even longer than that. My father being a womaniser predates Peter, and that's the problem with Angelo—'

'He's a womaniser too?' Jemima interrupted with a frown of dismay.

'I don't know about that.' Flora groaned and pulled a face. 'He's a gorgeous-looking guy and he's single and rich, so of course he's had a lot of women in his life. But he doesn't believe in love or romance. Strikes me he's a commitment-phobe.'

'Yet he clearly loves Mariska, or he wouldn't be so determined to bring her up, so I wouldn't give up hope on him yet. A child is a very big commitment for a single man to take on,' Jemima pointed out thoughtfully. 'He's also doing everything he can to support you and he clearly wants the triplets as well. Full marks for him on that score.'

'I'm not saying that he doesn't have an admirable side to his nature. I mean, it's obvious that he really likes kids,' Flora conceded grudgingly.

'And fancies the socks off you,' Jemima chipped in. 'Or you wouldn't be in the condition you're in now. He'd be keeping more distance between you if he didn't want a relationship with you. I think his inviting you to share his home with him is quite a statement for a so-called commitment-phobe.'

Encouraged by her friend to look at the more positive side of Angelo's invitation, Flora began to come to terms with her seemingly impulsive decision. She was starting to appreciate that something a good deal stronger than impulse had prompted her to accept Angelo's proposition. In her heart of hearts she recognised that, in spite of her fears, she did truly want to have the courage to take a chance on Angelo. He might often infuriate her but she did find him hugely attractive and stimulating company. He was the first man since Peter to make her feel that sense of connection and she wanted and needed to explore that in greater depth.

Three days after Jemima's departure, a professional firm arrived to pack and transport her most cherished belongings to Amsterdam, while special travelling arrangements were made for her dog and cat. Angelo rang most days but since he was very busy and often between meetings they would only have time to speak for the space of a minute so it was never a challenge to maintain a conversation. Flora was already feeling a good deal stronger since she had cancelled her remaining guest bookings and had spoiled herself with early nights and relaxing days. She was relieved when the worst attacks of nausea almost immediately receded and her appetite began to slowly recover.

Only three weeks after she had learned that she was carrying triplets, Flora arrived at Angelo's Amsterdam home.

Skipper, who had travelled over two days earlier,

raced to greet her with boisterous enthusiasm and she clutched his little squirming body below one arm while the driver who had collected her off her flight brought in her suitcase. Mango the cat, Angelo's housekeeper, Therese, informed Flora, was sleeping in his basket by the stove in the basement kitchen.

'He is being spoiled a lot. Therese adores cats,' Anke shared laughingly as she came downstairs holding Mariska.

The little girl held out her arms to her aunt in immediate happy recognition. Flora scooped the child into a loving embrace. All the agonies of insecurity and the misgivings that had tormented Flora since she had first agreed to move to Amsterdam fell away with her niece's first hug. As she held Mariska's solid weight to her and felt the warmth of her smooth baby cheek against her own, Flora finally believed that she had made the right decision.

A couple of hours later, comfortably clad in casual togs, Flora was happily sitting on a rug in the nursery building up brick towers with Mariska and toppling them again when she received an unexpected visitor.

An elegant platinum blonde, wearing a beautiful flowing top and trousers in a shade of grey that lent an even more flattering silvery hue to her hair and porcelain complexion, rapped lightly on the ajar door to attract Flora's attention and gave her a wide smile that showed off perfect teeth. 'I hope you don't mind me dropping in. I asked Therese if I could come up. When Angelo mentioned that you were arriving today I wanted to be the first to welcome you to our city,' she said brightly.

It was Bregitta Etten, whom she had first met in Angelo's house on the evening of the same day that she had conceived her triplets. Angelo and Bregitta had been on the brink of going out somewhere that night but Flora had never had the courage to ask what the beautiful blonde's exact relationship to Angelo was, and just at that moment not knowing made her feel distinctly uncomfortable. She scrambled upright while Mariska crawled round her feet and grabbed her aunt's trouser leg to haul herself into standing position on sturdy little legs. 'Thank you,' Flora responded a little awkwardly, while reaching down to pat the little girl's head soothingly.

'It's wonderful to see you with Willem's daughter... poor little girl, such a tragedy to lose *both* parents at once,' Bregitta sighed with rich sympathy. 'Of course, when Mariska has grown up she'll have a very large inheritance to help her come to terms with that tragic loss.'

Taken aback by that remark and its rather mercenary tenor, Flora frowned. 'Mariska...has an inheritance?'

A look of surprise flared in Bregitta's bright dark eyes. 'Mariska will come into her father's trust fund once she's an adult. Didn't you know that?'

Rosy colour warmed Flora's cheeks because she was embarrassed that it had not occurred to her that her niece would inherit and she also wondered why Angelo had neglected to mention it to her. Evidently Bregitta was much more informed about the van Zaal family's private financial affairs than Flora was and in the circumstances it was a slap in the face for Flora to be confronted head-on with that reality.

'Of course, had he had the opportunity Willem would

have wasted his inheritance, and Mariska, just like her father before her, is a heavy responsibility for Angelo to take on.'

Flora lifted her chin. 'I realise that Willem had his problems,' she commented, choosing her words with care. 'But he was kind, he loved my sister and I liked him.'

'I didn't intend to offend you,' Bregitta responded ruefully. 'We Dutch simply like to be frank.'

'Oh, no, you didn't offend me!' Flora proclaimed in haste, wondering why it was that she was finding it so hard to warm to the other woman's apparent friendliness.

Bregitta shook her silver-blonde head, her expression wry. 'I shouldn't have commented but Angelo already has so many weighty commitments in his life.'

'I wouldn't really know about that,' Flora admitted uneasily, wondering if she with her expected progeny fell into that demeaning category as well.

'Angelo just accepts it—his life has always been that way. When his father made such a disastrous second marriage, Angelo had to grow up fast, and then, of course, Katja's accident only made it worse.'

Katja? Who was Katja? Flora was hanging on her companion's every word and eaten alive by curiosity, for Angelo revealed few personal facts. The marriage between Angelo's father and Willem's mother had been a disaster? Why? And what on earth had happened to this Katja? It did, however, set Flora's teeth on edge that she should know so little while Bregitta evidently knew so much.

'Mariska is very lucky to have you and I'm sure

Angelo is extremely grateful for your assistance with her,' Bregitta commented, frustratingly moving the dialogue on in another direction after having whetted Flora's appetite for more information. 'Of course, a lot of women have recently offered Angelo help and advice with childcare. There is something so touching about a man trying to raise a little girl alone, isn't there?'

'I wouldn't know.' Flora could feel her face assuming a more and more wooden lack of expression. 'Angelo's the only male single parent I've ever met.'

'He's been positively *swamped* with offers of assistance. But then women have always found Angelo irresistible!' Bregitta pronounced with a rather pitying giggle. 'My husband used to tell me stories about when he and Angelo were boys together and even then Angelo was a total babe magnet!'

Suddenly Flora's tension ebbed and she began to smile. 'Your husband and Angelo are close friends?'

'The very best of friends…until Henk died last year,' Bregitta replied with a slight grimace.

'I'm sorry. I didn't know,' Flora responded, scolding herself for instantly wondering if the lovely outspoken blonde was of the merry widow variety.

'Henk was ill for a long time. Angelo was a wonderful friend to both of us.'

Relieved to establish that Bregitta was a friend rather than a more intimate connection, Flora nodded her understanding.

'Angelo said that you had been ill and needed rest and recuperation. How are you feeling?' Bregitta enquired with a sharply assessing appraisal.

'I'm feeling fine now.'

Unable to conceal her curiosity, Bregitta continued to study Flora closely. 'I hope it was nothing serious. Looking after a young child is very hard work.'

It dawned on Flora that, while Bregitta might have known about Mariska's inheritance, she was not aware that Flora was pregnant by Angelo. Her cheeks colouring again in a hot rush at that awareness, Flora shrugged off the comment and said nothing more while she wondered why she would have preferred to hear that Angelo had been more open about her condition. Was she afraid that his silence on that score meant that she was an embarrassment to him? Or that her moving in with him was such a casual arrangement on his terms that he had seen no reason to mention it to his acquaintances?

Shortly after Bregitta's departure, Angelo phoned Flora.

After asking her how she was settling in, his dark drawl sending little tingles of awareness down her taut spinal cord, he said casually, 'At this time of year I usually spend weekends at my country house. I'll understand if you prefer to remain in Amsterdam though because you've only just arrived.'

'I would love to see the house,' Flora broke in impulsively.

'Good. I'll make the arrangements and I'll join you there for dinner. I did intend to meet you at the airport but I'm afraid a crisis arose at one of the plants in India.'

Minutes later he had rung off, and Flora lifted Mariska and went off to pack a weekend bag. Anke packed for Mariska with the ease of long practice and mentioned how much she enjoyed the relaxed atmosphere at Huis van Zaal. In turn Flora wryly recalled her late sister's vehement complaints about how bored she had been when Willem had insisted that they visit his brother's country home the previous summer. Of course, Julie, she reflected wryly, had always been very much a city girl.

Flora enjoyed the drive out into the pretty countryside where herds of black and white Friesian cows grazed the meadows and windmills presided over the ever-present stretches of water. Her first view of Angelo's red-brick country seat through a line of espaliered lime trees took her breath away, for, in spite of its name, Huis van Zaal was a small castle complete with a pair of enchanting turrets and a wide moat studded with water lilies.

'I didn't realise that it was a castle!' Flora commented in surprise.

'It has been in the van Zaal family for over two hundred years,' Anke told her. 'My parents farm nearby.'

It was not a huge building and was less a fortress than a home, for, although it might have battlements, it also had shutters on the windows and sat in a lush green oasis of lawns and box-edged borders.

Skipper raced out of the car and had to be sternly recalled before his investigations took him for a dip in the moat. Greeted by a smiling older man called Franz, Flora was shown upstairs to a light-filled bedroom furnished with a magnificent four-poster bed rejoicing in sunflower-yellow damask drapes. Her face warmed as she wondered if she would be sharing the room with Angelo, but she soon discovered that there was no male apparel stored in the antique furniture. By the time she had applied a little make-up and put on a leaf-green dress that swirled round her knees, Anke had Mariska in the old-fashioned bath adjoining the nursery at the end of the corridor.

Flora was finishing off Mariska's bedtime story when Angelo arrived and as her niece vented a little shriek of excitement Flora fell silent at the sight of the tall, darkly handsome male in the doorway. His brilliant smile lit up his lean dark features and made her heart thunder in her ears. She watched him lift Mariska out of her cot and saw the delight on the little girl's face, recognising the bonds that had already formed between Angelo and her niece.

But while Mariska's attention was all for Angelo, his sapphire-blue eyes immediately sought out Flora. She was smiling, her vivid colouring and blooming silhouette accentuated by the backdrop of the pale curtains. She could not drag her attention from his tall, powerful physique. Angelo looked amazing in a dark, well-cut suit and a blue tie that picked up the stunning hue of his eyes. He really was gorgeous, she savoured helplessly, in thrall to the wicked hormones rampaging through her body in a floodtide of reaction.

'I'm afraid I'm much later than I hoped to be,' he confided in his husky, sexy drawl before bending his head to address Mariska in Dutch for a couple of minutes. Then he turned back to give Flora his full attention. 'I'm glad you're here. Very often I only see Mariska first thing in the morning and last thing at night.'

'Yet, even though I had much more time to offer her you were still determined to adopt her,' Flora could not resist reminding him.

His brilliant gaze cooled and his handsome mouth

tightened. 'Now she has both of us and hopefully the best of what we can both offer her,' he countered smoothly.

Made to feel mean for having made her less than gracious reminder, Flora reddened uncomfortably. But she could not forget that, even though in terms of time and attention she had much more to offer Mariska, Angelo had demonstrated very strong resolve in continuing to battle to become Mariska's sole legal guardian. For the first time she wondered if that resolve had been driven purely by his fondness for Willem's daughter. Or by the conviction that he, rather than Flora, would make the better parent. A pang of hurt cut through Flora at the thought that she might have been tried and found wanting by him without ever being aware of the fact and she hastily suppressed the feeling, irritated that she was so sensitive where Angelo was concerned. Why hadn't he made her aware that her niece was to inherit her father's substantial trust fund? That mysterious oversight on his part niggled at her, for she could think of no good reason for his silence on that issue.

While Angelo excused himself to go for a shower, Flora descended the gracious carved staircase alone. Franz showed her into an elegant drawing room and offered her a drink, which she refused. She stood at the French windows, which overlooked the charmingly picturesque gardens.

'What do you think of Huis van Zaal?' Angelo asked as he came through the door to join her.

'It's got wonderful warmth and character,' Flora responded and her voice shook a little when she focused on his tall, well-built figure. With his black hair damp and spiky, and clean-shaven, he had the sleek bronzed face of a fallen angel and the level of his charisma just took her breath away.

'I'm glad you like it here. It's my childhood home and I'm very attached to it.' His dazzlingly blue eyes flared, his handsome mouth tautening as her attention lingered on him. 'Don't look at me like that.'

Warm colour swam into Flora's cheeks but still she couldn't look away from him and the heat of desire simmered in the pit of her stomach like a taunt, because she had believed that she was stronger than that, stronger and fully in control. Only now was she learning her mistake. 'Why not?'

'It ties me in knots and I'm struggling to be a civilised host and follow the accepted script,' Angelo murmured huskily. 'And we're about to have dinner to celebrate your arrival.'

'I'm not hungry right now,' she heard herself object, as she was infinitely more eager for physical contact and the strength of her own longing shook her.

'*Dios mio*, you're tempting me, *enamorada mia*.' To drive home that point, Angelo crossed the room in a couple of strides and reached out to haul her unresisting body up against his lean, hard physique.

Behind her breastbone her heart started to crash like cymbals being banged together and a dark insidious excitement began to build, along with a wild sense of anticipation. Without further ado, he brought his mouth down hungrily on hers and her hands closed over his wide shoulders to keep her upright. That first kiss was nothing short of glorious. His raw masculine passion smashed down her barriers and desire sweet and painful and all pervasive engulfed her in a floodtide of reaction. But she wanted more, much more, and it was terrifying and exhilarating at one and the same time.

'You use a lot of Spanish in your speech,' she mumbled abstractedly when he finally released her reddened lips and allowed her to breathe again.

'It was my first language.'

'Not Dutch?' she queried, surprised by the information.

'My Spanish mother never learned to speak Dutch fluently, which was why we used her language within the family,' Angelo told her before returning to pry her lips apart with the seeking thrust of his tongue and then delve deep when she opened to him, with a raw groan of appreciation rasping low in his throat.

And that was the magical moment when she discovered that even a second kiss from Angelo could make her tremble and yearn with a force of desire she had not known possible. Every kiss set her on fire for the next so that she squirmed against him, desperate with the driving need for closer contact.

'Feel what you do to me, *querida mia*,' Angelo husked, a hand on her hip crushing her to him so that she could feel the urgency of his erection even through their clothes. 'I want you so much it hurts to exercise restraint.'

'Don't be restrained—why should you be?' Flora broke in helplessly, loving the way he shuddered against her with an arousal he could neither hide nor deny, for in that field at least it seemed that they were equals.

His bright eyes had the crystalline glitter of diamonds. 'I need you,' he growled.

And that admission was like the magic talisman that unlocked the gate to the treasure house of trust inside Flora. The word 'need' meant so much more than mere wanting to her. It had depth, hinted at staying power, suggested closeness on other levels, in short was everything she had dreamt of receiving from a man. She found his wide, sensual mouth again for herself and revelled in his unashamed passion for her.

Angelo bent down and swept her up into his arms to carry her out to the stairs.

'We *can't*!' Flora gasped, torn between horror and laughter at his single-minded audacity.

'We can do whatever we want to do, *enamorada mia*. There are no restrictions and there is no right or wrong way for us to be together.' As he spoke his carnal mouth nudged against the sensitive cord of her slender neck and followed it down. She quivered helplessly as he teased and nuzzled the nerve endings below her smooth skin. He knew things about her body that she didn't know and she rejoiced in his carnal skill and confidence.

He laid her down on the four-poster bed in her room and slipped off her shoes.

'You know I'm not made of glass,' Flora told him awkwardly, conscious that he was holding back. 'I won't crack or break.'

'I know.' Angelo flung her a hooded look of dark sexual promise, his jewelled eyes a bright gleam behind the thick black frosting of his lashes. 'But going slow is sexier and I've waited a long time to get you back. I want to enjoy you and I want you to enjoy me, *querida mia*.'

Suddenly Flora was breathless and wreathed in

blushes as self-consciousness threatened to eat her alive. That day on the houseboat there had been little time to think about what they were doing; they had succumbed to a mad, impetuous bout of passion. It was a little different from lying back on a bed watching Angelo unbutton his shirt. The edges parted on the corrugated muscularity of his washboard-flat stomach and just as quickly watching became a sweet seductive pleasure. He strolled back to the bedside and gently turned her to access the zip on her dress, stringing a line of kisses across her shoulders as he eased the dress down to her waist.

I've waited a long time to get you back. She tasted that admission afresh, loving it, for it suggested she was special and that he would have wanted her even though she had not fallen pregnant. She was stunned by how much that idea meant to her and finally appreciated that by some insidious means Angelo had long since succeeded in getting below her skin. For the first time in a very long time the prospect of caring for a man didn't frighten her.

Angelo lowered her to the pillows and removed the dress, pausing to run boldly appreciative eyes over her full breasts cupped in a pretty white and blue polka dot bra. Before the packing was done, she had binned her sensible pregnancy bras with the thick straps and popped out to go shopping for new lingerie. From his reaction, it appeared to have paid off handsome dividends. But within the space of a minute the bra was gone and the ample bounty of her curves was spilling into his hands instead. A startled gasp parted her lips as he stroked the soft mounds and rolled the distended pink nipples between his fingers before lowering his handsome dark head to suckle the stiff crests. She was so sensitive there that she moaned helplessly, her breathing shallow and erratic as the pulse of heat between her thighs burned hotter than ever.

He peeled off her remaining garments and touched her where she could almost not bear to be touched. He teased the exquisitely tender flesh with erotic skill and she shuddered in his embrace, so hot and wet and eager she couldn't find words for the intensity of the hunger that possessed her. He tugged her to the side of the bed so that her legs dangled free. He spread her thighs and she felt shockingly exposed and she shivered, fingers knotting nervously into the silk spread below her hands.

'You shouldn't,' she told him shakily between gritting teeth, for every natural instinct and modest fibre was urging her to push him away and reject such intimacy.

Angelo surveyed her with fierce intensity and it was a look that brimmed with ravenous desire. 'I *must*,' he contradicted. 'I love your body, *querida mia*.'

He slid upright and dispensed with his trousers and boxers in one impatient movement. The hard thick contours of his erect manhood bore witness to his declaration and at the sight of his arousal Flora felt absolutely weak. He came back to her, pushing her knees to her chest to explore the slick damp pink folds she would have hidden from him, had she not been limp with the desire he had already awakened. He slid a finger into her tight passage while he used his tongue on the little pearl at the heart of her. As the sweet, tormenting pleasure began to build, she moaned out loud and jerked, her hips giving way to a feverish twisting motion. She had never reached such a high of sensation and when she could no longer withstand that sensual assault she went spinning over the edge of it with a keening cry and fell into the depths of writhing ecstasy, her every fantasy fulfilled.

'Oh…Angelo.' Struggling even to speak, Flora gasped as Angelo kissed her and rearranged her limp body on the bed before returning to her with urgent intent.

His bold shaft nudged at her damp entrance and then sank deep. He groaned out loud in satisfaction. 'You're so tight, *querida mia*…so wonderfully tight.'

'I've not had a lot of practice at this,' she admitted, exulting in the sensation of her inner muscles stretching to accommodate him while wondering if it was humanly possible to die from an overload of pleasure.

Briefly, Angelo frowned down at her as if he was seeking her meaning, but her eyes had closed and at that instant she was in the mood to say no more. Her head rolled back as he gripped her hips to surge deeper into her tender channel, answering her need with the long sure strokes of his urgent possession. Quivering with delirious delight, she arched up to him, catching his rhythm and ready to reach for the stars again.

The sensations were getting sharper, the fiery ache in her pelvis stronger, and then her body jerked and flew into orgasm and she was crying out and shaking in receipt of the indescribably intense waves of devouring pleasure. For a minute or two she lay with her skin hot and damp with perspiration, cradled in the warmth of his embrace.

'You were more than worth waiting for, *querida*

mia,' Angelo declared, smoothing her hair back from her flushed face with gentle fingers.

Her lashes lifted and she focused dreamily on the lean, darkly handsome face so near to hers. She shifted closer still and hugged him, all the deep affection of her nature surging to the fore in the aftermath of that powerful physical release. She wondered when it had happened, when exactly she had fallen head over heels in love with a guy she had continually told herself she felt nothing for. That day on the houseboat? The weeks afterwards when she had denied herself even the pleasure of speaking to him on the phone for longer than thirty seconds? The afternoon she had learned she was pregnant and he had responded with laudable cool and the immediate offer of his support? In truth Flora didn't know when or even how she had fallen for Angelo van Zaal, only that just then it felt good to have taken that leap of faith and for once not to expect the worst from a man.

'You said I was worth waiting for. How long is it since you've had someone else in your life?' Flora asked boldly, already seeking to establish boundaries and know where she stood.

Angelo vented a roughened laugh and dark colour demarcated his superb cheekbones. 'I haven't been with anyone else since I was with you.'

Flora gave him a dazzling smile in reward and thought that he was showing great promise in the relationship stakes.

As if wary of having made that admission, Angelo added with a frown that drew his ebony brows together, 'I don't know why. Other women have seemed less appealing...somehow. Perhaps it's because—'

'No, don't spoil it by trying to explain it!' Flora urged, laying her forefinger against his wide mobile lips in a silencing gesture.

'I don't think I could explain my recent weakness for a particular tall, spirited redhead but it does seem to be working out very well indeed, *enamorada mia*,' Angelo murmured with satisfaction, and he sucked her finger into his mouth and laved it with his tongue while watching her with slumberous shimmering blue eyes awash with hot expectation.

Heat swept through Flora even before he kissed her again and she responded with a fervour she could not restrain. Everything had fallen into place when she was least expecting it to do so and they had shifted into the role of lovers quite naturally. No longer was she holding back, checking out every word she spoke in advance and searching for double meanings in everything he said. She had abandoned the intense caution that had guided her and kept her heart whole and safe for several years and without that defensive barrier she did feel vulnerable. Yet turning her back on the uniformly low expectations she had of the male sex and putting Angelo into a category all of his own also left her free to enjoy being happy for a change.

And, in the aftermath of yet another bout of passionate lovemaking, Flora was on a high such as she had never experienced with a man before. Within the hour they sat down to eat in the panelled dining room, the home of a wonderfully colourful collection of Chinese porcelain, stored in elegant white cabinets that kept the room looking airy and light. Undaunted by their earlier non-appearance, Franz had put together a chicken salad and an array of mouth-watering desserts for their enjoyment. Skipper, who snored like a little steam train, was noisily asleep beneath the table, though once the food was served he stirred a little to maintain a mistrustful if drowsy watch on Angelo's every move.

It was only while Flora was toying with a dessert that was a little too sweet for her taste buds that she remembered what she had meant to ask Angelo to explain earlier. Glancing up from her plate, she casually tucked a straying strand of coppery hair back behind her ear. 'I have something I've been meaning to ask you…'

Angelo studied her with a lazy smile. 'Ask away.'

Flora straightened her slim shoulders. 'Why didn't you tell me that Mariska was going to inherit your stepbrother's trust fund?'

And the instant she asked, she knew she had strayed into dangerous territory, for Angelo perceptibly tensed, his brilliant eyes veiling to sharp arrows of blue while his lean strong face shuttered. 'Who told you about that?'

'Bregitta Etten called in to wish me well this afternoon and she mentioned it,' Flora explained in a rush of nervous energy. 'Naturally it felt a little weird that I had no idea that my niece was in line to come into Willem's money! Why was I the last to be told?'

A heavy laden silence stretched between them like a treacherous sheet of ice that could not be crossed and mentally she told herself off for being so fanciful…

CHAPTER EIGHT

'I saw no reason to discuss the matter with you,' Angelo fielded with measured cool. 'After all, surely it was fairly obvious that my stepbrother's trust fund would go to his only child?'

'Yes, I suppose, if you think about it from that angle perhaps it was rather obvious. But it didn't occur to me because while Willem was alive he didn't have access to that money,' Flora pointed out, unimpressed by his explanation, indeed smelling a rat and a cover-up in his guarded response. 'I didn't consider it… I genuinely had no idea.'

'It is a private matter. Bregitta shouldn't have broached the subject with you,' Angelo remarked flatly.

'But she did and it made me feel rather foolish—why was I kept in the dark?' Flora enquired a little more forcefully, for, unless it was her imagination, Angelo's handsome mouth had curled with a hint of scorn when she had contended that she had had no idea that her niece was an heiress. '*Why*, Angelo?' she repeated with greater emphasis.

Angelo expelled his breath in an impatient hiss and sprang upright to his full intimidating height, forcing her to tilt her head back to look up at him. His brilliant blue eyes collided with hers and held her gaze stubbornly fast. 'I didn't know for sure whether you knew about her inheritance or not, but I was concerned that your desire to adopt Mariska could be influenced by the reality that she will one day be a rich young woman. What's more, were you now to win custody of her you would be legally able to apply to the trust fund for a sizeable income with which to raise her.'

Flora was stunned into silence by those twin admissions. She wanted to believe that she had misheard him or taken his words up wrong, but he had left her no margin to dream of error. As always, Angelo had spoken with concise crystal clarity. Incredibly, the man she had just spent most of the evening in bed with, the man whose babies she carried in her womb, saw no shame in admitting that he thought that she might be a gold-digger. And not only that, a calculating gold-digger so shameless and hard of heart that she might be willing to use an innocent child's birthright to enrich herself. It was equally apparent that he would not have trusted her with access to Mariska's inheritance. Flora was absolutely horrified that he could see her in such an appalling light.

She thrust back her own chair and stood up, the oval of her flushed and taut face reflecting her sense of angry disbelief. 'What on earth gave you the impression that I might only want my niece because she stands to come into a substantial bequest? What did I ever do to leave you with that idea? What did I say?' she demanded emotively.

Angelo spread fluid brown hands in a wry gesture. 'You didn't need to do or say anything, Flora. Before

Willem even married your sister, I was acquainted with, not only her past history, but also yours,' he confessed grimly.

Her brow indented. 'You're talking about that private investigator's report that you mentioned you'd commissioned,' she guessed, and her heart began to sink as she immediately deduced the most likely source of his reservations about her character.

'I'm aware that you slept with your married boss three years ago and tried to blackmail him to gain a lucrative bonus,' Angelo informed her flatly.

Flora reeled back a step as though he had slapped her, but what he had just thrown in her teeth was much worse than a slap, for he had resurrected a distressing episode that she had believed had long since been laid to rest, even though it had not had a satisfactory conclusion from her point of view. To be confronted by that same episode again years later, and by someone she cared about, was an agonisingly humiliating and painful blow for her to withstand.

'That is not what happened, Angelo,' she pronounced with quiet dignity as Skipper emerged from below the table and stationed his little black and white body protectively by her feet. 'Those malicious allegations against me were made in an employment tribunal hearing, not in a court of law, and they were not proved either. I did not sleep with my boss, nor did I try to blackmail him!'

His lean hawkish features stamped with unhidden distaste, Angelo made a decisive movement that dismissed the thorny subject with one lean brown hand. 'It was some years ago, Flora. I'm well aware that what is past is past and that young people in particular can and do learn from their mistakes and change...'

The target of that extremely patronising response, Flora experienced a shot of adrenalin-charged rage, which coursed through her with such powerful effect that she was surprised that she didn't levitate off the floor. She ground her teeth together in an effort to think before she spoke but it was hopeless. She felt both betrayed and gutted. The most traumatic episode of her life had been dug up by the guy she believed she loved and she felt cheated by his distrust and gutted by his low opinion of her as a person.

'I will never ever forgive you for this, Angelo,' she said shakily, targeting him with tempestuous emerald-green eyes that shone as bright as stars in her pale face. 'How dare you stand in judgement over me for something that I didn't do? How dare you condescend to suggest that people change? I've got older but I haven't changed one little bit. All I learned from that tribunal was not to trust people, and that when things get really *really* tough you're very probably going to be left standing alone!'

'I don't think we should try to discuss this when you're so upset,' Angelo breathed deflatingly, registering that Skipper, a perfect illustration of Flora's mood, was now growling and baring its teeth at him.

'*You* brought it up, *you* threw it at me!' Flora reminded him with spirit. 'You can't deny me the right to defend myself.'

'I had to explain why I was reluctant to be more frank about Mariska's financial status. I am not denying you the right to defend—'

'Of course, it's none of your business. My past is none of your business either and I can only wish that I had kept my present in the same category!' Flora flung in furious rejection of the choices she had recently made and Skipper, picking up on his owner's increasing tension, started to bark noisily. 'But when you had such a poor opinion of me, why didn't you mention it before now? How dare you lure me over to Amsterdam to live when you think so little of me? You deceived me by staying silent…'

'Tell the dog to stay out of this,' Angelo urged with a sardonic look down at the small canine bouncing excitably round her feet and barking so loudly that Flora was now virtually shouting to be heard. 'I had no deceptive intent.'

'Well, isn't that a surprise? Once again you try to take the moral high ground. But it doesn't matter what you think this time. I firmly believe that I was lulled into a false sense of security and deceived by you!' Flora slammed back at him in wrathful condemnation.

Angelo studied her with hard blue eyes, every inch the global steel magnate whose ruthlessness had earned him substantial achievements. 'I had no choice but to remain silent. How could you expect me to challenge you about your unsavoury past while you were carrying my children and you were unwell?'

Flora was trembling. Even his choice of words was revealing. Her *unsavoury* past. Without any input from her on that issue, he had clearly tried her, judged her and condemned her as guilty. At least she now knew why she had always suspected that he disapproved of her and disliked her. Angelo van Zaal had decided that she was not to be trusted even before he first met her. She need not have worried about trusting him when it was clear that he had never trusted or in fact respected her. Indeed the very existence of her pregnancy had forced him to swallow his misgivings about her character and attempt to form a relationship with her. Was it any wonder that he had decided that the most he could offer to share with her was a bed? No doubt had he been in a position to do so, he would have happily kept his distance from her and her sleazy past, she conceded wretchedly.

'I hate you,' Flora breathed thickly, struggling to enunciate the harsh words of rejection and alienation that seemed to come from the very depths of her being. 'And I'm leaving!'

As Flora made her way towards the door Angelo was suddenly there in front of her, blocking her exit like a massive stone wall. 'I won't let you leave—'

'I'm not giving you a choice!'

Angelo stared down at her with brooding force, jewelled blue eyes shimmering like a heat haze over her defiant and resolute face. He took a step closer as if to dare her to do her worst. 'I won't allow it!'

'Newsflash, Angelo—I don't need your permission to leave you!' Flora flung wrathfully. 'So, get out of my way and stop trying to crowd me!'

'*Por Dios*, I insist that you calm yourself down,' Angelo instructed in a low growl of explicit warning.

And Flora just lost her temper at that ringing admonition, for she fiercely resented being treated like a misbehaving child when it was very much his fault that she had found herself in such an untenable situation. Did he honestly believe that they could simply continue as though nothing had happened? That she could just live with the news that he believed that she was greedy and untrustworthy with money?

Her hurt and her anger combined in an explosive melding of emotion. She flung herself at him with knotted fists and thumped his big wide shoulders to fully illustrate her point. '*Move!*' she yelled at the top of her voice.

'*Madre mia!*' Angelo vented in a savage undertone as he shifted before the overexcited Skipper could bite his ankle. 'What the hell are you playing at?'

In the hail of her dog's frantic bout of barking, Flora froze, her balled fists dropping back down to her sides, because somehow she had never envisaged Angelo losing his renowned cool. But Angelo's jaw line had taken on an aggressive angle and his electrifyingly blue eyes were luminous with outrage. All of a sudden, a silent Angelo was channelling anger like an intimidating force field.

'You provoked me beyond bearing,' Flora slammed back at him in her own defence because an apology of any kind would have choked her. 'And you're still in my path!'

'Where I will be staying until you have got a grip on your temper...or should I say tantrum?' Angelo derided in a cutting undertone.

'Get out of my way!' Flora launched at him afresh, any desire to be reasonable crushed at source by that crack, although she did admonish Skipper for the racket he was making and the little dog finally fell silent.

Lean, darkly handsome face rigid with displeasure, Angelo stepped back with infuriating reluctance. Flora flashed past him to head for the stairs. Halfway up, she almost tripped over Skipper as her anxious pet got below her feet and that instant of hesitation almost unbalanced her into a fall. As she clutched at the balustrade with a hissing gasp of fright Angelo braced his hands on her shoulders from behind and steadied her.

'You're okay. I've got you,' he said fiercely.

Unable to tolerate even that throwaway remark, Flora twisted her head round. 'But that's just it! You haven't got me and you never will again! You actually believe I'm after your money, even though I've flatly refused to touch a penny of it!' she reminded him doggedly. 'I was totally independent until you pushed your way into my life and insisted on interfering—what was that all about? Why didn't you just leave me alone?'

'Lower your voice,' Angelo growled.

'No!' Flora fired back her refusal without hesitation because shouting at him was making her feel better by giving her an outlet for the emotions dammed up inside her. She didn't want to stop fighting with him either because she dimly recognised that when the argument was over she would find herself standing amid the debris of a wrecked relationship and she was in no hurry to reach that sobering point.

'You've screwed up my life!' Flora continued between gritted teeth as she stalked back to her bedroom where Skipper shot below the bed and whined, disturbed by the raised bite of their voices and the furious tension still in the air.

'*Dios mio*, my life has been turned upside down as well,' Angelo retaliated.

Flora's head spun, for she had not expected a response to her accusation. 'Try carrying triplets and see how much worse you feel!' she stabbed back, determined to have the last word.

Incensed by her complete obstinacy, Angelo watched Flora throw herself down in a heap on the still disordered bed. 'You're very pale. You need to be resting, not fighting with me,' he told her grimly.

Flora reared up again on both elbows, green eyes full of rancour. 'Were you expecting me to jump up and down with glee when you told me you thought I was a gold-digger, ready to fleece my baby niece?'

'I refuse to lie and pretend that I wasn't suspicious of your motives when you first applied to adopt Mariska,' Angelo declared, standing his ground.

'But even so, in spite of your suspicions you *slept* with me!' Flora raked back at him with a look of fuming feminine censure and incomprehension.

A flare of colour scored the sculpted line of his high cheekbones, but he stared her down, refusing to admit fault on that score. 'When did I say that I was perfect?' Angelo traded in his dark deep drawl.

Flora looked daggers at him and then rolled over to push her face into the welcome coolness of a pillow. What a mess, what a gigantic mess it all was! She wanted to cry and scream but she would do neither in front of him, so she pummelled the pillows with her fists instead. She was here in his home, she was available and because she was pregnant he was currently stuck with her, so that was probably why he had insisted that he still wanted her and that their relationship should be an intimate one. But their ties were the result of happenstance rather than planning. He might still desire her body, might want to have sex with her, but that was *all*. There was nothing deeper to his feelings for her. What an idiot she had been to lower her guard, let herself soften and fall in love with him! When had she forgotten that she knew next to nothing about men and invariably got it wrong with them? How had she overlooked the fact that she was dealing with a very rich, very handsome womaniser more used to taking than giving?

'Just leave me alone,' Flora urged from the muffling depths of the pillow. *'Please...'*

Angelo clenched his even white teeth and closed strong brown hands over the footboard of the bed where he flexed his fingers impatiently on the solid wood. 'Women usually prefer honesty...'

Flora rested her hot cheek on her hand and half turned her head to squint at him, tousled copper hair settling in a glorious silken tangle round her shoulders. 'Oh, we just say that because it sounds good...but we don't want honesty unless it's the kind of stuff we want to hear,' she told him tartly.

Angelo breathed in deep and slow and then swore below his breath anyway, while his knuckles showed white on the footboard as he held it too tightly for comfort. 'I didn't intend to hurt or upset you—'

'Oh, shut up,' Flora interrupted. 'What you intended has nothing to do with this. There's no wriggling out of it either. You had serious reservations about my character and you concealed them from me. In the circumstances that was very unfair. Do you honestly think I would have come here to live if I'd known what you really thought of me?'

'The jury's still out on what I really think about you.'

Flora shrugged her slim shoulders in a gesture of sublime disinterest on that score. '*So?* You think I'm about to tie myself up in knots struggling to win your good opinion? I couldn't care less,' she claimed defiantly, flipping over onto her back to study him with accusing green eyes. 'But there's one fact which you ought to know. I was a virgin when you slept with me that day on the houseboat. You didn't notice but that fact does make it impossible for me to have staged a sleazy affair with my boss three years ago.'

'A virgin?' Angelo repeated in a seriously shocked undertone, his strong black brows pleating into a brooding frown as he stared searchingly down at the composed oval of her face. 'I was your *first* lover?'

'Virgins don't all go round wearing helpful labels to warn off predatory men,' she said flippantly, annoyed by his scepticism over her confession and deciding there and then to tell him no further secrets when he was clearly such an undeserving cause.

'I'm not a predator. I had no reason to think that you might be that innocent. I was also aware that you were engaged at one time,' he reminded her, clearly still reluctant to accept that she might have been as inexperienced as she had claimed.

Flora grimaced and compressed her lips. 'Peter respected me,' she fielded.

At that response, Angelo studied her with scantily veiled incredulity.

'Well, that was his excuse.' Her grimace had acquired a pained edge and she screened her gaze from his keen appraisal, for the dialogue had become too personal for comfort. The hurt that her one-time fiancé and former best friend had inflicted had left a wound that had still not fully healed. As she had her selfish father before him, she had trusted Peter and where had that got her? He had let her down when she most needed him. And in spite of the fact that Peter had been a big part of her life for several years she had not heard a word from him since they had parted.

Angelo was studying her troubled expression fixedly, his strong jaw line clenching hard as her gaze continued to evade his. 'You still care for your ex-fiancé, don't you?'

'We were good friends until we broke up.'

'That's not an answer.'

'You don't do romance or commitment. You're not entitled to any more of an explanation,' Flora told him loftily.

Angelo gave her a look that had the pure cutting edge of a steel blade. 'I'll see you in the morning. You must see that you can't leave. What about Mariska? And your health?'

Her brain suffered from overload when he mentioned the little girl that she loved and her pregnant state in one loaded and unnecessary reminder. Turning her back and leaving Angelo might feel doable in the rawness and pain of being confronted by his true opinion of her, but the concept of walking away from Mariska straight away threatened to tear Flora apart. She closed her eyes tightly, shutting him out completely, and she didn't move again until she heard the door close on his departure.

Angelo might be a whizz at the realistic stuff, but there was nothing practical about the powerful emotions engulfing Flora. She had fallen head over heels in love with Angelo and now she had to get over him again, detaching herself from both love and sexual hunger. And, as even looking at Angelo's lean bronzed darkly handsome features sent a dizzy jolt of craving through her that she despised, recovering from that weakness promised to be a big challenge. The bottom line was that Angelo van Zaal had hurt her badly and inside she felt deeply hurt and foolish.

What sort of a man had chosen to believe a tabloid scandal about her rather than seek out the truth? Of course, how had the investigator chosen to represent that particular episode? Probably with his own assumptions wrapped up as facts. And hadn't Peter, who had supposedly loved and known her through and through, chosen to disbelieve her side of the story as well? That old 'no smoke without fire' cliché had certainly not worked in her favour. Peter and his family had been appalled by the sleazy tabloid stories depicting her as a woman scorned out for revenge and their engagement had died on that funeral pyre of suspicion and embarrassment. Although, if she was honest, Flora ruminated wryly, her relationship with Peter had been under strain even before that.

When they had first met at university Flora had been firmly set against premarital sex and live-in relationships and determined to protect herself from that kind of potential disillusionment. Her mother, after all, had lived

with her father for years before he reluctantly deigned
to marry her and his unwillingness to be bound by one
woman had enabled her father to cause havoc in many
female lives.

Peter, who had studied accountancy while Flora had
studied business at university, had come from an old-
fashioned family and her uncompromising views had
impressed him. His loyalty was soon stretched thin,
however, when Flora won a job that paid more than
twice what he was earning as well as offering the prospect of substantial bonuses. His mother and sisters had
made snide comments about what a career woman Flora
was turning out to be.

Unhappily for Flora, that high-flying job had swiftly
turned into a nightmare. The only woman on an all-male
team, Flora had found herself working for a despotic
boss, who demanded that she work impossible hours
and who cracked smutty jokes and made continual embarrassing comments about her figure. She had tried
hard to be one of the boys and laugh his behaviour off,
but the comments had ultimately led to inappropriate
touching and sexual suggestions. A married man in his
thirties, Marvin Henshall had had considerable success
with such tactics with other female staff and Flora's
resistance had only made her a more desirable target.

When the pressure Henshall was putting her under
became unbearable, Susan, one of the women in the
administration office, had confided that she had been
subjected to a similar campaign. Together the two
women had made a complaint about Marvin to Human
Resources and, from that moment on as their grievances
gathered pace through official channels, Flora's life in

the office had become intolerable, with the other male staff ignoring her while Marvin ensured that her most successful client accounts were gradually parcelled out to her colleagues.

Peter had pleaded with her to find another job, but there had been nothing offering a commensurate salary and Flora's pride had refused to allow Marvin Henshall's victimisation, bullying and sexual harassment to go unpunished. Unhappily, however, her tribunal case had come badly unstuck when Susan backed out on her at the last possible moment and Marvin made up a sordid if credible story that was difficult to disprove. Humiliatingly, Flora had lost the case.

Her reputation destroyed by the amount of mud flung at her in the newspapers, Flora had bitterly regretted not just leaving her employment and seeking out another job. That Angelo should tax her with that tribunal case and the ludicrous accusations laid against her outraged her sense of justice and resurrected her need to be independent. She would never look at another man again, she promised herself fiercely, for sooner rather than later every man she let into her life let her down.

The following morning, Flora's breakfast was served to her in bed. She had suffered a restless night and just to remind her that she was still not back in full control of her pregnant body she was horribly sick. What remained of her strength was sapped from her by the shower she took. Fully dressed, but weak of limb and bathed in perspiration, she lay back down on the bed to recover. Her spirit as feisty as ever, though, she used the opportunity to rearrange her thoughts and fine-tune them, because she was determined to resolve her situation with

Angelo and find a viable alternative to their current living situation.

She found Angelo much more easily than she had expected in so spacious a household. With Mariska tucked comfortably below one arm, he was standing in front of a portrait on the wide galleried landing and talking in Dutch to the little girl.

'Flora…' Breathtakingly handsome in well-worn denim jeans and an open necked shirt, Angelo swung round to settle azure-blue eyes fringed by luxuriant black lashes on her.

As heat formed low in Flora's pelvis and her nipples pinched to tingling tightness, warm colour blossomed in her cheeks. In spite of the fact that she was still angry with him, that rush of sexual response was unnervingly strong. Her niece beamed at her but continued to cling to Angelo and Flora tried to be a bigger person and not mind the fact. She joined them in front of a large gilt-framed picture of an elegant lady. 'Who is she?'

'My late mother. I can't show Mariska a portrait of Willem's mother because my father didn't commission one.' His wide sensual mouth quirked. 'And even if he had, I wouldn't have given it wall-space!'

Flora glanced at him. 'You didn't get on with your stepmother?'

'She was a shrew, always picking fights with friends and family. She bullied poor Willem unmercifully. People avoided her. Sadly my father didn't have that power.'

'Why on earth did he marry her?' she asked on their passage down the gracious staircase.

'He was very happily married to my mother, who died

when I was ten. He assumed that he would be equally happy in a second union and remarried hastily without truly knowing Myrna. He was very unhappy with her,' Angelo confided grimly. 'I still believe that the stress of living with that woman brought on the heart attack that killed him.'

'Bad marriages can damage and hurt the children involved,' Flora conceded, entering the drawing room, which overlooked the lush gardens and rejoiced in an array of inviting seating. 'I've told you about my history and Julie's.'

'*Sí*, her mother was your father's girlfriend.'

'But only one of them. Dad spread his favours far and wide,' Flora admitted wryly and she reached out to accept Mariska, who was by now holding out her arms in welcome to her aunt. She smiled as she received an enthusiastic hug and stroked the little girl's soft cheek with warm affection as she settled down on a sofa with her.

Angelo viewed them with veiled eyes. 'I was planning to offer you a tour of the local sights today.'

Flora froze, thinking that only Angelo would dare to try and ignore their explosive and bitter argument the night before and move on so smoothly. 'Not just at the minute. I think I should take it easy after all the travelling I did yesterday.' Seeing renewed tension enter his lean masculine features at that refusal, Flora continued awkwardly, 'About last night…'

'Lying doesn't come naturally to me,' Angelo remarked drily. 'I'm too accustomed to the freedom of speaking my mind.'

Flora stiffened, for it was clear that he had no regrets

about having admitted his reservations about her as a person. But then, who would ever have dared to call him to account over his bluntness? She could well imagine that women eager to please the very rich and very handsome billionaire had let even the most wounding candour slide past without protest. Being labelled a gold-digger had, however, left Flora in an unforgiving mood and she had no desire to placate him. 'I now know where I stand with you and I can't regret that. I think I know how we can work this out.'

For a big powerful male Angelo moved with extraordinary grace, but at that assurance he stilled by the window, his simmering tension obvious in his stance. His dazzling blue eyes were bright as peacock feathers between the ebony fringes of his lush lashes. *'How?'*

'Well, obviously we don't go on trying to live together as we started out last night. The words "frying pan" and "fire" come to mind. We just forget that angle,' Flora proposed in a clipped undertone, stress and concern at how he might react to her proposition tightening her facial muscles. 'You seem to own very large houses, so living separately below the same roof shouldn't be a problem in the short term.'

It might well have been her imagination but the healthy glow of vitality that Angelo's vibrant skin tone usually lent him suddenly seemed strangely dull and absent. 'Is that truthfully what you want?'

Flora released her breath in a slow sigh. 'Right now I don't want any complications or stress. I want to concentrate on Mariska and these babies I'm carrying.'

Angelo jerked a shoulder in an eloquent shrug. 'I

can't fault you for that, but I had hoped that we could *discuss...*'

Flora's green eyes were suddenly as flat and hard as green jade and her chin came up. 'I don't want to discuss anything with you. I know what you think of me and that made it clear to me that there was no future for us as a couple,' she framed doggedly. 'I may need your support right now because I'm carrying triplets but I would prefer you to treat me only as a friend or...er... housemate from now on.'

Angelo was frowning. 'If that is honestly what you want?'

Her teeth ground together because he was making it very obvious that he had little experience of a woman saying no to him and that he could not quite credit that she might know what she was doing.

'It has to be what you want as well!' Flora snapped back, her temper leaping because even though he had not opposed her his whole attitude seemed to imply that she was being somehow unreasonable. 'You admitted that my pregnancy had turned your life upside down.'

His very blue eyes burned like sapphire jewels above his hard cheekbones. 'But it doesn't necessarily follow that that is a bad thing.'

Flora dragged her attention from his all too charismatic appeal and folded into a bristling ball, with Mariska cradled sleepily on what lap she still had to offer. 'Oh, come on, you had it *all* before that day your luck ran out on the houseboat,' she muttered with a snide edge that she could not suppress. 'The beautiful women, the choices, the lack of ties or commitment. That kind of relationship was never ever going to suit me and it's better to recognise our differences now *before* the babies are born.'

A muscle pulling tight at the corner of his unsmiling mouth and his bright eyes veiled, Angelo inclined his arrogant dark head in grudging acceptance. 'It's very important that you can feel happy and secure here. I will respect your wishes. But, for the record, I think you're making a major mistake for both of us.'

Mistake or not, Flora had all the painful satisfaction of knowing at that instant that she had hoped he would fight with her and *for* her, wanting and demanding more than she thought it sensible to give. Of course his ready agreement merely pointed out what intelligence had already tried to tell her. He cared about what might happen to her but his feelings ran little deeper than ensuring she stayed strong and healthy for the sake of the babies she carried. *His* babies and, for a male as fond as he was of children, that was always likely to be a very big deal.

Hot prickling tears stung Flora's eyes and she lowered her lashes so that he would not see and she hugged Mariska in consolation. She might have fallen hard for Angelo van Zaal, but she had no intention of giving him cause ever to suspect that mortifying truth. From now on, she would be brisk, businesslike and as cool as a cucumber in his radius…

CHAPTER NINE

'You look marvellous,' Bregitta Etten chorused with her usual girlish enthusiasm. 'The expression "blooming" comes to mind.'

Flora resisted an uncomfortable urge to smooth her lilac dress down over her sizeable bump; she was almost seven months pregnant and pretty large in the tummy stakes and standing for long periods was a strain for her. Unhappily, Bregitta always made Flora feel ill at ease. 'Do you mind if I sit down?'

'Of course not. I can see you need to. It must be exhausting carrying all that extra weight around,' the beautiful blonde carolled, planting her reed-slender body down beside Flora on a hard gilded sofa. Both were attending an event that was being staged in a grand public building offering more splendour than comfort. 'It is so unfortunate that Henk and I were not blessed with children.'

'That is sad.' While striving to remain pleasant in the face of Bregitta's fake friendliness, Flora endeavoured not to look around to see where Angelo was. The benefit was being held in aid of one of the charities that Angelo headed up, an organisation that raised funds for brain-damaged children. As Angelo knew virtually all the

guests present and had given a rousing speech he was
very much in demand. He had asked her to attend as
his partner and since he rarely asked her to accompany
him anywhere she was determined not to be clingy or
needy.

'I'm an old-fashioned girl,' Bregitta murmured sweet-
ly, eyes as cast down as a dewy teenager's in her show
of modesty. 'I would have to be married before I could
take the risk of having three children at once.'

'Would you?' Flora simply laughed, too used to the
blonde's needling little digs to even react. She had long
since worked out that Bregitta cherished very personal
designs on Angelo and would have been deeply resentful of any woman sharing his home. The news a couple
of months earlier that Flora was also carrying triplets
had shocked Bregitta rigid and left her as aggrieved as
though Angelo had been stolen from her.

That rather amusing recollection made Flora's soft
full mouth quirk, for she was convinced that Angelo did
not share Bregitta's intimate aspirations with regard to
their friendship. Furthermore, while Angelo might not
have told his friends that he was to become a father
before Flora's arrival, he had positively bragged about
the fact since then. Although he had failed to be equally
frank about the fact that they were only living together
now for the sake of convenience, she cherished no doubts
about his enthusiasm for his impending fatherhood. And
as a daily witness of his relationship with her niece,
Flora had come to accept that Angelo was one of those
special men who truly loved children and enjoyed their
company.

During the past four months, Flora had regained her

health but as her pregnancy progressed she had become more physically restricted in terms of what she could do. She got tired much more easily and her back and hips ached if she walked too far. Getting down on the floor to play with Mariska was impossible now, as was sleeping the night through with three very active babies moving about inside her. Yet she was always aware that the closer her triplets got to term before she brought them into the world, the safer they would be.

Natalie had put her in touch with a consultant obstetrician in Amsterdam, who maintained a careful weekly check on her condition. Jemima also rang her friend regularly to be reassured that she was all right. But Angelo, more than anyone, had provided Flora with unparalleled support. Ironically, that acknowledgement made Flora feel almost unbearably sad, for the more she learned about Angelo van Zaal, the more she knew why she loved him. She might have initially been attracted to him because he was downright gorgeous and very sexy, but he was also courteous, considerate and always ready to listen if she was worried about anything. Indeed she had no grounds for complaint whatsoever because Angelo had given her exactly what she had asked him for: her privacy.

Usually they only mixed when Mariska was present and, with the single exception of tonight's charity benefit, the several outings they had shared had included the little girl. In every way that mattered, Flora and Angelo currently led separate lives. Angelo spent most of the day at his office and about one week in four travelling abroad. When he was at home they occupied separate rooms and often ate at different times as well.

As the weeks wore on Flora began to wonder if she had made a drastic misstep in her overwhelming eagerness to save face. Angelo was leaving her alone just as she had requested and she had to assume that there were now other women in his life. She could hardly expect a male with a high-voltage libido to abstain from sex and live like a monk. He was, however, being admirably discreet about any other interests. Even so, his discretion was not a comfort for her because jealousy was eating Flora alive if he so much as looked at another woman.

And although Angelo appeared content, Flora was very much aware that she was feeling lonely, unhappy and insecure. Her pride had certainly come before her fall, she acknowledged ruefully. She recognised that her refusal to challenge his belief that she was a gold-digger head-on had put a wall of misunderstanding between them, which he was understandably reluctant to tackle in the current climate. Naturally he did not want to distress her or make her more hostile to him. He could scarcely be expected to understand that as she had got the chance to know him without the unsettling influence of sexual attraction always taking front-row billing he had finally earned her trust. With Angelo, she had come to accept, what you saw was what you got. There was nothing false, nothing hidden, no polite pretences or lies. He was as far removed from a lying, cheating philanderer of her late father's ilk as any man could be and had a much stronger character than Peter had ever had.

'You are so brave, Flora. How can you be so calm?' Bregitta asked in measured disbelief, lifting her pencilled brows in emphasis of the point. 'In a few months you'll have four children under two years old and

Mariska is already running around and creating havoc as toddlers do. I'm afraid I cannot picture Angelo in so domestic a role.'

'He's crazy about kids,' Flora fielded confidently.

'Any man in my life would have to want me more than any children I might have,' Bregitta informed her without hesitation, 'but with Angelo that could be a problem for you.'

Stung by that all too perceptive comment, Flora made no response for on that score she had no comment to make. Angelo was only with her, after all, because she was pregnant, and once her babies were born they would have to come to some other convenient arrangement, which was highly unlikely to be one in which they continued to live below the same roof. Soon, she recognised painfully, even living within easy reach of Angelo on a daily basis would just be a fond memory. Then wasn't it time for her to speak up in her own defence? Was he content with the way things were? And if he wasn't content, why hadn't he said anything?

'If you ask me, the only woman who ever held Angelo's heart was Katja.' Bregitta sighed. 'And as she's the one who got away, metaphorically speaking, who else is likely to make the grade?'

Flora was confounded by the idea that Angelo might once have loved and lost a woman, or might even have been rejected, but she was too proud to question Bregitta, who she was well aware was a troublemaker. Instead Flora looked across the room to where Angelo was laughing with another gorgeous blonde in a skimpy red cocktail frock that showed off her pert breasts and slender thighs. A sharp and painful pang darted through

Flora because her own once shapely figure had vanished.
Were Angelo and the blonde sharing an innocent joke?
A flirtation? Or was Flora, in fact, seeing lovers using
the opportunity to enjoy a brief moment of intimacy in
public? That she had no idea of what she was seeing
or indeed what was happening in that part of Angelo's
life hurt her and underlined the gulf she had opened up
between herself and the man she loved. For, in spite of
all her efforts to the contrary, she loved him more than
ever, she conceded ruefully.

Angelo joined her ten minutes later. 'You look sleepy,'
he murmured softly.

Lie, she wanted to shout at him. Tell me I look sexy
or beautiful or anything other than tired even if it is
a barefaced lie! But she swallowed back her discomfiture over her excessively sensitive reaction while he
stretched down a hand to help her upright with as much
care and concern as if she were an ailing and elderly
lady. Suddenly she hated being pregnant and longed to
be small and blonde with pert breasts and a tiny waist!
I'm so shallow and superficial to feel that way when I'm
pregnant, she thought shamefacedly, but with all her
heart she was longing for the smallest sign that Angelo
could still find her attractive.

Jolted by the strength of that craving, Flora was furious with herself and she went straight up to bed, turning down the offer of the supper that Angelo suggested
they share. She was cutting off her nose to spite her
face, she reflected ruefully as she settled heavily under
the covers. In spite of the uneasy mood she was in she
slept for a couple of hours, though only to waken to
the sensation of what felt like a game of football being

played inside her womb. She lay still for a few moments, her palm lightly covering her swollen abdomen and the little movements she could feel with a tenderness she couldn't help. A pang of hunger assailed her about then and although she tried to ward it off, she failed and her mind was soon awash with images that merely revved up her taste buds. Minutes later, she finally climbed out of bed and reached for her robe.

In the basement kitchen Mango purred continuously and wound himself round her legs while Skipper continued to snore in his basket. The big traditional kitchen in the Amsterdam house was a wonderfully warm and inviting place. Delft tiles covered the massive chimney-piece while cream-ware crockery was displayed on the painted dresser and polished copper utensils on the walls. In one corner an antique walnut grandfather clock slowly ticked out the time.

'*Dios mio*…I thought I heard someone…'

At the sound of Angelo's voice Flora turned her bright head and saw him framed in the doorway. Skipper loosed a sleepy bark and then scrambled out of his bed to go and welcome Angelo while his mistress watched with jaundiced eyes. She had discovered that Skipper was very much a man's dog and prone to lying in wait at the front door waiting for Angelo to come home. How Angelo had accomplished the feat of overcoming Skipper's distrust and replacing it with downright devotion, she had no very clear idea, for she had yet to see any sign of Angelo doing anything more than giving Skipper the most cursory pat on the head.

Unlike her, Angelo was still fully dressed, although he now sported a pair of faded jeans with his ruffled white dress shirt and had removed his jacket and tie. Her cheeks reddened because she knew her hair was as tousled as a bird's nest. She indicated the salad sandwich she was in the midst of putting together. 'I should have had supper,' she admitted wryly.

'I know better than to say, "I told you so",' Angelo drawled, lounging back against the massive scrubbed pine kitchen table with his lean powerful thighs spread in a relaxed attitude.

'That doesn't always stop people saying it. Are you hungry?'

'Thanks, but I ate earlier. I stayed up to do some work.'

'Sometimes the babies move around so much they wake me up. I don't sleep very well,' Flora admitted, sinking down into Therese's rocking chair by the stove to eat her sandwich. 'I've been thinking too...'

'What about?' Angelo prompted.

Flora made herself withstand the appeal of the sandwich for another moment and breathed in. 'I think it's time I told you about that tribunal case.'

Watching her eat, Angelo frowned, a wary light in his bright blue eyes that immediately put Flora on the defensive. 'You can believe or disbelieve me—that's your choice,' she added with more than a hint of challenge.

'Naturally I would like to hear your side of the story.'

A little of her discomfiture ebbed and she began to tell him about the wonderfully well-paid job she had won within weeks of gaining her business degree from a top university.

'But why didn't you complain the instant your boss

began harassing you?' Angelo was quick to enquire with a frown.

'At first I was worried that I was being over-sensitive and misinterpreting his signals. I think a lot of women feel like that in an all-male work environment when there's a lot of pressure not to make a fuss about anything,' she confided tautly. 'I was trying very hard to fit in and I didn't want to get a name for being difficult. When Henshall's approaches became more blatant I started worrying about how a complaint about him sexually harassing me—and he was *very* highly thought of in the company—would affect my career.'

Angelo was frowning. 'That is not how you should have felt…'

'I'm not talking ideals here…I'm talking about what it was like on the ground. Many of the people I was at university with hadn't even found jobs. I knew I'd been given a terrific opportunity and I was desperate not to screw it up.'

'It was your boss who was screwing it up, not you. If what you're telling me is true, how on earth did you lose the case?'

Flora grimaced. 'Two things ensured that I lost that tribunal case. The other woman making a complaint with me against Henshall got cold feet and withdrew it, so I was left without supporting evidence. The second was Henshall's claim that I'd been having an affair with him and it had turned sour because he'd stayed with his wife and refused to give me that bonus.' Flora's oval face was pale and strained. 'That provided the sleaze angle that attracted the attention of the tabloid newspapers and resulted in some very nasty headlines on my account.

Many people chose to believe Henshall's story, because nobody could believe that a married man would own up to an affair when there hadn't been one—'

'Why do you think he pretended that you and he had had an affair?' Angelo asked levelly.

'Because he was afraid he would lose his job if I was able to prove that he was a sex-pest. He earned a huge salary, so lying and striving to discredit me by blackening my reputation made sense from his point of view. His wife supported his appearances at the tribunal every day for the same reasons. He'd had at least half a dozen work affairs and she must have known what he was like.'

'Your engagement broke up around the same time,' Angelo recalled.

'After the newspapers got involved, Peter and his family felt that being associated with me was too much of an embarrassment. But I did get that wretched bonus in the end,' she completed ruefully.

Angelo could not hide his surprise on that score. 'You *did*?'

'I had earned it fair and square on performance and the company knew it and paid up, but only after the publicity had died down. I still have it in the bank... untouched,' Flora admitted.

'Not much of a consolation in the circumstances, I imagine,' Angelo remarked, helping her upright as she began to rise slowly from the chair.

'It wasn't,' she agreed.

'I'll see you up to bed,' Angelo murmured.

Flora buttoned her lips on an immediate urge to tell him that she would manage fine on her own. Fiery

independence was all very well but keeping Angelo at
arm's length was no longer what she wanted. As he drew
close a whiff of the exclusive citrus-based cologne he
used wafted over her and unleashed an intimate tide
of images. She remembered the hot passion of that
wide sensual mouth on hers, the sure tantalising touch
of those lean brown hands, and a knot of pure sexual
tension tightened between her legs. Distracted by her
embarrassing thoughts, she tripped over her feet in her
haste to enter her bedroom and Angelo closed his arms
round her from behind to steady her.

'Take your time,' he urged softly.

But there was hardly any time left for them to be
together, she thought painfully. She knew that her obstetrician was wavering on the brink of instructing her to
take bed rest for the remainder of her pregnancy. Once
the freedom to move around was taken from her, she
would be even more isolated and separate from Angelo
than she already was.

Angelo slid her robe off her shoulders with an ease
that reminded her just how at home he was with a woman
in a bedroom and her cheeks burned. As jumpy as the
proverbial cat on hot bricks, she lay down on the bed
and as he began to move away she found herself reaching for his hand in a movement that took her as much
by surprise as it appeared to take him. He swung back,
his dark lashed gaze positively welded to the sight of
her hand on his, the tension in his lean sculpted features
palpable. 'Don't go…' she framed without even being
aware that the plea was brimming on her lips. 'Yet,' she
threw in stilted addition.

Angelo glanced at her. His brilliant blue eyes had a

crystalline glitter behind his lashes and he settled his
long powerful body down on the edge of the bed. 'Are
you feeling all right?'

Her teeth gritted. She had that familiar feeling of
inadequacy she often got in his radius of late: a near
overpowering urge to sob and scream in frustration. She
asked him to stay with her and the only reason he could
come up with was that she might be ill or in the grip
of her nerves. Of course, she was hardly a beguilingly
sexy proposition just at present, she reasoned ruefully,
striving to be fair to him.

'I'm all…r-right,' she started to say, only a kick from
one of the babies stole her breath and made her stammer.
'Just a kick,' she explained, pressing the heel of her hand
against her stomach.

'Would you mind?' His interest clearly caught,
Angelo rested his palm down very close to hers, evidently in the hope of feeling one of the babies move
again.

'Of course I don't mind,' Flora lied because, in truth,
she was now even closer to sobbing in frustration. Lying
very still, she stared down at the rising mound of her
stomach and wondered what on earth she had been playing at in even dreaming of acting the temptress. Once
again the triplets had effortlessly contrived to take centre
stage.

As Angelo felt a baby kick a look of wonderment
transformed his lean, darkly handsome features. She
saw his pleasure and felt mean for minding that she was
simply a human incubator for the babies Angelo could
hardly wait for her to have. Had she tried, she could not
have found a keener father-to-be. It was a wonder he

hadn't got married years ago and already fathered a little tribe of offspring, she thought ruefully. Of course, no doubt he had learned the lesson of being cautious when his father had got badly burned in his rushed second marriage. Furthermore, there was no denying the fact that Angelo valued his freedom and had fought to preserve it from the outset of their acquaintance. Had he felt differently about the mysterious Katja, whom Bregitta liked to hold up as an unassailable rival? Flora only wished that she had not chosen to overlook his love of his freedom at the outset of their relationship, for caution might have saved her from heartbreak.

'You're amazing,' Angelo murmured in a tone of husky admiration, looking right down into her eyes with those dazzlingly blue eyes that made her mouth run dry and her shameless heart thunder in her ears.

She wanted so badly to touch him that she had to curl her fingers into her palm to stop herself from stretching out her fingers. Her breathing grew shallower and more audible, her breasts swelling until the tender tips were prominent while heat and moisture pooled in her pelvis. He held her gaze and the atmosphere buzzed with electric tension. For several taut moments she was unable to reason because she was wholly in the control of her rebellious hormones and the hunger he could ignite.

Angelo removed his hand from her stomach and tugged up the linen sheet to cover her. 'It's late. I mustn't keep you awake,' he said with precision, his voice deep and rough-edged, and he straightened and switched out the bedside light. 'Don't forget that you have an appointment with the obstetrician tomorrow afternoon.'

Moonlight was spilling welcome clarity round the

edges of the curtains. Her heart in her mouth, Flora watched Angelo walk to the door and her sense of mortification was so intense she could think of nothing to say in return. What had she thought or even hoped? That he might kiss her? Show some hint of sexual interest or even regret at the distance between them? What a foolish dream that was to cherish when she was about as fanciable as a stuffed turkey!

Tears stung Flora's wide open eyes in a hot burning surge and inched slowly down her cheeks. She blinked furiously and one of the babies kicked and she just burst out crying then, pushing her face into the pillow to muffle the noise that she was making while reflecting that she would look even worse in the morning with reddened swollen eyes.

When she awoke late the following morning after a restless night, it was to the beep and flash of a text on her phone and she stretched out a drowsy hand to lift it from the bedside table. Once she realised with astonishment that the text was actually from her former fiancé, Peter Davies, she sat up in surprise and curiosity to read it immediately. Having bumped into a mutual friend, Peter texted that he was shocked at the news that Julie had died and that Flora was currently living in Amsterdam with her niece. Flora was equally taken aback to learn, when she responded, that Peter now worked for a Rotterdam-based shipping company in London, was currently in the Netherlands at a conference and was keen to meet up with her before he returned home.

Consumed by curiosity over why he should have chosen to contact her after so long, Flora discovered

that Peter would be heading back to London that very
evening and she agreed to meet him for coffee before
he left for the airport…

CHAPTER TEN

ANGELO accompanied Flora to her appointment with the obstetrician. Her face fell when the doctor told her that he thought she would benefit from bed rest for what remained of her pregnancy.

'You're doing very well but, at this stage, every extra day that your triplets remain unborn is another day for them to develop into bigger and healthier babies,' Mr Wintershoven pointed out with sympathy. 'I would have advised you to come into hospital now, but with the care Mr van Zaal is able to provide you can safely remain at home.'

'It'll be so boring lying there,' Flora sighed as she and Angelo left the exclusive hospital where Mr Wintershoven had his consulting rooms. She felt guilty for even voicing that complaint because she knew that the obstetrician's advice was sensible for a woman in her condition.

Angelo looked down at her, blue eyes bright as sapphires in his lean bronzed face. 'I will keep you entertained. We'll go from here straight to your favourite bookshop and we'll buy films as well...'

'I can't—I meant to tell you earlier but I forgot to

mention it. I'm meeting someone this afternoon,' Flora
told him.

'Who?' Angelo enquired baldly.

Slight colour tinged her cheeks. 'Peter texted me.
Apparently he was attending a conference in Rotterdam
this week and we're going to meet for coffee before he
travels home.'

'*Peter?*' Angelo repeated in a startled undertone that
made her glance up at him and notice the tautness of
his strong jaw line. 'Peter Davies? Your ex-fiancé? He
was in Rotterdam this week?'

Flora smiled. 'Yes, he's an accountant with a shipping
company that has its head office based there. Isn't that
an amazing coincidence?'

'It is. I wasn't aware that you were still in contact
with him.'

'I wasn't. Once I left London we lost touch with each
other. He texted me right out of the blue after running
into a mutual friend who told him about Julie's death,'
Flora told him with a grimace.

Angelo was standing very still by the limousine. 'Of
course, he would have known your sister.'

'Yes, but to be truthful they never got on that well,'
Flora recalled wryly; Peter had resented the time and
attention she gave her sister.

Angelo watched her climb into the car and smooth
her trousers over her knees. 'I'll come with you.'

Flora gave him a startled look. 'Why would you do
that?'

Angelo compressed his handsome mouth into a
line, a tiny muscle tugging at the corner of his perfectly moulded masculine lips. 'I don't like you going

anywhere alone at present. I would be happier if I went with you.'

'That's ridiculous. All I'll be doing is walking into a coffee shop to sit down and then coming back out again when I'm finished,' Flora pointed out drily.

'I'd still prefer to accompany you,' Angelo told her stubbornly, evidently impervious to gentle courteous hints.

'Well, you *can't* come! You won't be welcome,' Flora told him bluntly. 'Peter and I couldn't discuss anything personal if we wanted to with you present.'

Clearly far from reassured by that statement, Angelo stared broodingly down into her resolute face. 'You really do want to meet up with him, don't you?'

Flora nodded unembarrassed affirmation. Curiosity motivated her more than any other reason, but she didn't see why she should share that fact with Angelo. After all, what was it to him if she met up with her ex-fiancé for a friendly coffee and a chat? Hadn't he enjoyed complete freedom to see other women for months on end? And difficult and painful though it had been to remain silent and not interfere in his life, Flora had not once weakened in her stance, or asked him a single nosy question.

The conversation over, she emerged from the limo outside the designated coffee shop and, uneasily aware of Angelo's annoyance at the novel sensation of having his wishes utterly ignored, Flora gave him a warm reassuring smile. But his brilliant eyes remained grim and his handsome mouth and strong jaw line stayed rigid. Feeling like a ship in full sail in the blue maternity top she wore, Flora headed into the café.

Peter was already there waiting for her. Although she immediately recognised him, she also noticed that his hairline had begun to recede and he had put on weight. The instant he saw her he leapt to his feet and began telling her how sorry he had been to hear about what had happened to her sister.

'I knew you would be very upset. You and Julie were so close,' Peter declared. 'And when I heard about it and found out you were living in Amsterdam, I just *had* to see you! The way we parted is still on my conscience...'

'It's a long time ago now,' Flora commented mildly, relieved to discover that even the sight of a wedding ring on Peter's rather podgy hand didn't move her to regret the past in the slightest.

As Flora turned to choose her seat Peter's attention dropped to her bump and he looked at her in flagrant surprise. 'You're pregnant?'

Flora could not help laughing at his expression. 'Why not?'

'You're not married.' Peter dropped his voice to make that comment as if afraid others might be embarrassed by that statement of fact.

'And you are. We've both changed and moved on,' Flora declared comfortably, pausing to order her coffee. 'When did you get married?'

Peter turned brick-red. 'A few months after we split up,' he admitted. 'Her name's Sandy; we worked together.'

Flora smiled. 'And yet you never mentioned her to me.'

'I know. I felt very guilty about keeping quiet but what would have been the point of telling you?'

'If I'd known there was someone else, I wouldn't have felt our broken engagement was my fault,' Flora responded with wry assurance. 'I felt guilty about all the bad publicity my tribunal case had attracted and the effect it had on you and your family.'

Peter winced. 'I was the one in the wrong, Flora. I'm sorry. I didn't have the courage to tell you how I really felt and I used that tribunal fiasco as an excuse to break off the engagement. I'll always be ashamed of that.'

'Never mind,' Flora said generously and she sipped tranquilly at her coffee.

'I let you down and I'll always regret that but we weren't right together. I felt more like your brother than your boyfriend,' Peter confided with a look of discomfiture. 'Somewhere along the line we lost that essential spark and I handled it very clumsily.'

It was as though a little cloud had cleared away from Flora's view of the past. She saw the truth of what he had just said. Their relationship had been based more on friendship than passion and, as time had gone on, the attraction between them had waned rather than deepened. Peter had first recognised the problem because he was attracted to Sandy, whom she also noted he had wasted little time in marrying. She wished he had been more honest because she did not think she would have felt quite as rejected had Peter simply admitted that he had fallen for another woman.

'We weren't suited,' she told him, striving not to wonder if too much exposure to her was a turn-off for men in general. Was that what was amiss with Angelo?

Was he indifferent to her now? Had familiarity while she lived in the same household simply led to contempt?

'You were always too headstrong and ambitious for me.' Peter shook his head. 'Sandy makes me feel good about myself—'

'Let's leave it there,' Flora advised drily before he could make any more less than tactful comparisons.

Peter asked her about the father of her children and confided that he was already the father of a year-old son. She enjoyed his surprise when she mentioned her triplets and thirty or so minutes wound up pleasantly enough before they went their separate ways. She travelled back to Angelo's mansion in a taxi and wondered why she had beaten herself up over Peter's defection for so long. By the time they had left university they had outgrown each other and become more of a habit than a couple in love, but she had been so bound up in her challenging new job that she had failed to appreciate that truth.

The baby bag already sitting packed in the hall reminded Flora that it was the weekend and time to head to Huis van Zaal again. She hoped that Angelo was not expecting her to take to her bed that very day and stay on in Amsterdam because she loved the relaxing pace of the weekends. If Angelo was free to come down to his country house, business was never allowed to act as a distraction within those ancient walls. But sadness touched her too, for although the weather was still bright and sunny the cooler temperatures of autumn were already in the air and now Angelo was a less frequent visitor to his country home.

'Where's Angelo?' she asked Anke in the nursery.

'I think he went to see Katja so he shouldn't be too

long,' the nanny informed her cheerfully as Mariska toddled over to Flora to show off the new dress she was wearing. A happy confident child, Flora's niece seemed to have suffered no lasting harm from her less-than-ideal early months with her troubled parents.

And there and then, Flora almost asked Anke who Katja was, because she knew the young nanny would satisfy her curiosity without making a production out of it. But it also occurred to her that Bregitta had deliberately made a point of twice mentioning Katja, which very likely meant that there was nothing at all questionable in the relationship. Katja might well be ninety-five years old and perfectly respectable. Bregitta, after all, enjoyed making Flora feel insecure and would have been even happier to know that she had contrived to cause trouble between Angelo and the mother of his unborn children.

An hour later Flora was paying lip service to bed rest by lying on a padded lounger enjoying a glass of home-made lemonade while she basked in the early autumn sunshine. Mariska and Skipper were happily engaged in chasing the same ball tirelessly round the garden. Flora, however, was painstakingly counting her blessings. Angelo might not be in love with her, but he would be a very good father to their children and no doubt in time she would get over her constant wish and need for him to be something more than that. Four children, she thought, just a little daunted by the prospect as she registered the amount of noise that Mariska could make without any backup at all. When Anke asked if she could take the little girl to visit her parents' farm with her that afternoon, Flora agreed and let her weary eyes slide shut.

'Flora…?'

Flora lifted her lashes and focused dreamily on Angelo, her green eyes unusually soft. Tall, dark and gorgeous, he was poised only a few feet away, casually clad in well-cut trousers and a pale shirt that made a perfect frame for his bronzed skin and black-as-jet hair. She tilted her head to one side while she studied him, admiring the sleek planes of his high cheekbones, the classic patrician set of his nose and the beautifully modelled perfection of his wide masculine mouth.

'You're staring at me,' Angelo said softly.

Her cheeks flared with colour and as she met those very blue eyes of his her mouth ran dry. Blinking rapidly, she began to sit up, a process that was as slow and difficult for her with her cumbersome body as standing up in a hurry. Within seconds, Angelo was by her side and rearranging her more comfortably.

'How was Peter?' Angelo enquired coolly.

'He hadn't changed much.' Reluctant to run her former fiancé down or discuss what he had shared with her, Flora fell uncomfortably silent.

Angelo surveyed her with an odd intensity that she could almost feel like a touch on her skin. 'I have a question to ask you,' he imparted tautly.

'Go ahead,' Flora advised, hoping it didn't relate to Peter and taking a sip at her lemonade in an effort to seem composed.

'Will you do me the honour of becoming my wife?' Angelo asked levelly.

Flora glanced up at him in shaken disbelief and

somehow contrived to choke on her drink, breaking down into a fit of coughing that led to him banging her on the back to aid her recovery. Eyes still streaming in the aftermath, she mopped them with a tissue and tried frantically to work out where the marriage proposal had come from. He was asking her to marry him! *He was actually asking her to marry him.* After weeks and weeks of sharing the same roof without the smallest intimate contact, he was suddenly asking her to be his wife and she could not credit it. Stunned, she focused on his heartbreakingly handsome and very serious features and registered that he was definitely not joking. 'I…I… er…'

'I appear to have taken you by surprise,' Angelo breathed tensely.

'You've really shocked me… I mean, I definitely didn't see this coming over the horizon,' she mumbled unevenly, scarcely knowing whether she was on her head or her heels.

Angelo dropped down on the chair beside hers and reached for her hand. Brilliant blue eyes sought out hers. 'I would be proud to call you my wife.'

Flora tugged her fingers reluctantly free. 'Even though you think I'm a gold-digger?'

'Only a stupid man would get to know you as well as I know you now and still think you capable of such a motivation…I am *not* a stupid man, *tesora mia.*'

Flora was not so easily soothed. 'It's all very well saying now that you've changed your mind about that, but why has it taken you so long to tell me so?'

His lush black lashes semi-screened his gaze from her keen scrutiny. 'I had made you so hostile that I was reluctant to open the subject again in case I made matters worse. I'm not very good at eating humble pie either,' he admitted with gritty reluctance.

'You're as stubborn as a rock,' Flora pronounced without apology, studying the fierce tension etched into his hard masculine features.

'I should have had that tribunal experience of yours checked out again. Unfortunately it wasn't important enough to me when I first met you, but it was a mistake to accept what proved to be speculation as fact and to allow it to colour my judgement to such an extent.'

'I was very upset when I realised that you had always had a low opinion of me and why,' Flora admitted ruefully.

'I did finally have further enquiries made,' Angelo confided with gravity. 'It may be a consolation for you to learn that eighteen months after your departure from that company where you worked, Marvin Henshall was sacked for gross misconduct. There were fresh allegations of sexual harassment laid against him by a new employee.'

Flora was disgusted to hear that her former boss had found yet another victim but relieved that allegations against him had finally been made to stick and that he had paid the price for his behaviour. 'I'm glad that no other woman will have to go through what I went through again,' she murmured with heartfelt sincerity.

'I'm sorry that you had to suffer that way and that I took so long to admit what I believed I knew about you. You were right,' Angelo declared, his lean, strong face serious as he made the admission. 'It was unfair of me not to give you the chance to speak up in your own defence. My only excuse is that our relationship was already tense and I was afraid to put it under more strain.'

'You mean, I was pregnant,' Flora translated heavily.

'That only influenced me after I realised you were pregnant and unwell,' Angelo countered levelly. 'Prior to that point my only interest was in you and, right from the start, I didn't want to accept that our stolen afternoon on the houseboat was the most we would ever share.'

Her lashes lifted, her interest ensnared by that declaration, and she studied him with questioning cool. 'You wanted more?'

'*Dios mio!* Didn't I immediately ask you to spend the weekend with me here? Of course I wanted more. I lived my whole life through and I never once felt as alive as I did with you on that boat!' Angelo delivered in an undertone raw with the strength of his conviction. 'It was different; together *we* were different, even when we were arguing, and I'd never experienced a connection like that with a woman before.'

For the first time, Flora appreciated that she might have allowed the very fact that she was pregnant to get in the way of a closer understanding between them. In fact she too had been guilty of making far-reaching assumptions. 'I thought you were only interested because I fell pregnant.'

'How could I fake being interested and why would I do that anyway?' Angelo dealt her a bewildered look as Skipper dropped his ball at his feet.

'Because you felt it was the right thing to do when I was carrying your children...'

'I would never have invited you to share my life if I hadn't wanted you for yourself. To do otherwise would have involved us both in a relationship that could only have come to a painful conclusion.'

Pushing her hands down on the arms of the lounger, Flora got up and slid her feet back into her shoes to walk away a few steps. She had found it hard to believe that he truly wanted her and her pride had not allowed her to accept support from a man only offering it out of a sense of duty.

'When I first fell pregnant I wouldn't let you help me. I honestly thought that you only wanted to help because you felt you *had* to,' Flora told him in a troubled admission.

'I needed and wanted to help you but you made it so difficult. Sometimes it annoys me that you're so proud and so determined to be independent,' Angelo confided levelly.

'I'm a freeloader who's been living off you for months!' Flora proclaimed with spirit. 'Where's the independence in that?'

'You're no freeloader. You may live in my home but when have you ever even gone shopping at my expense?' Angelo prompted in frank exasperation as Skipper nudged his shoe with the ball. 'You won't spend my money—what am I going to do with you?'

Flora studied him warily from below her feathery lashes. 'Why have you asked me to marry you, Angelo?'

His jaw line squared. 'Believe me when I say that it is for all the right reasons.'

'Because we're going to have four children between us in another few weeks?' Flora shot at him.

Angelo laughed out loud, his irreverent grin chasing the serious aspect from his bronzed features. 'No, oddly enough that hasn't once entered my thoughts.'

Her brow pleated because she was baffled by that claim. 'It...*hasn't*?'

'Should I be ashamed to admit that the only two people in my thoughts are you and I?'

'No, not ashamed, but you're still not answering my question.'

Angelo bent down and lifted Skipper's ball to throw it. The little terrier went racing madly across the lawn and bounced across a box-edged border. Angelo studied Flora with narrowed blue eyes and a rueful expression that tugged at her heartstrings. 'I'm asking you to marry me today because I panicked when you went off to meet Peter. I was planning to wait until after our children were born before I proposed—'

'You panicked about Peter?' Flora cut in blankly. 'What's that supposed to mean?'

'The obvious. I was afraid that you still had feelings for your former fiancé and I didn't want you meeting up with him again.' Angelo compressed his handsome mouth. 'I was jealous. Okay?'

'Of...Peter?' Flora gasped incredulously, barely able to compute the concept that he could be jealous when she was so heavily pregnant. 'You were jealous of Peter...even with me looking as I do now?'

'You still light my fire, *tesora mia*,' Angelo intoned huskily, reaching for her hands and tugging her towards him. 'Why not his?'

'Because, for one thing…' Flora hesitated before continuing '…Peter and I never managed to light a fire in the first place and that was why we broke up. Are you serious? You still find me attractive looking like this?'

'*Por Dios*…very much,' Angelo asserted in a low-pitched growl of confirmation that sent a shimmy of desire dancing down her taut spinal cord.

Her eyes had opened to their fullest extent. 'But you haven't even kissed me—'

'You asked me to treat you like a housemate,' he groaned.

'You were supposed to argue with me when I said that but you didn't, so I assumed it didn't matter to you.'

'Of course it mattered. I'm not a block of wood!' Angelo exclaimed feelingly, releasing her fingers to cup her cheekbones and then lift his hands to run his fingers lightly through the fall of her hair. 'Have you any idea how hard it's been for me not to touch you?'

'No…'

And then he kissed her and the amount of pent-up passion and longing he contrived to put into that single kiss almost blew Flora away. Reeling from the effect of it, she leant up against his lean, powerfully aroused body and smiled secretly against his shoulder. Now she believed him. Now she knew that she had been blind and it was one of those rare occasions when she was happy to have been proved wrong.

'Even sharing the same bed with you would be an incredible thrill,' Angelo confessed raggedly. 'Nothing else is possible right now but that doesn't matter.'

'I thought "amazingly good sex" was my main attraction?'

'I've gone way beyond anything that basic. If I had realised that I was your first lover, I would have been a lot more diplomatic. Unfortunately I was trying too hard to be cool,' Angelo confessed with an almost shame-faced expression, pressing her in the direction of the house. 'Are we getting married?'

'Give me one good reason why,' she urged, her lips still tingling from that passionate kiss. She was very much open to persuasion.

'I love you. I love you so much that I can't imagine my life without you,' Angelo informed her as naturally as if he had already told her that every day for a year.

Flora turned shaken eyes on him. 'You told me that you don't do romance or commitment.'

'Well, I should have added the proviso...at least not until the right woman comes along,' Angelo incised silk-ily, closing an arm round her narrow spine. 'And you are, without a doubt, my perfect match. I'm a strong personality but so are you. I don't intimidate you.'

'You do annoy me though,' she muttered helplessly while trying to come to terms with the heady idea that he might love her.

'We bring out the best and the worst in each other. We're both stubborn, proud, impatient...'

Flora touched the arm he had curved round her. 'Get back to the love bit!'

'Equally bossy and we both like our own way.' Angelo slung her a wolfish smile. 'When are you going to answer me? I'm offering you everything you said you wanted.'

Flora came over all shy. 'I'm thinking it over.'

Angelo dug into his pocket and produced a small jewellery box, which he flipped open. 'Engagement ring...'

'Wow!' Flora exclaimed, watching the sunlight ignite a river of fire in the emerald and diamond cluster. 'I love it!'

He came to a halt in the hall and lifted her hand.

'It won't fit!' she wailed. 'My fingers are swollen!'

With an air of solemnity, Angelo discovered that for himself and slid it onto her little finger instead. 'I'd like to get married in the local church where my parents took their vows.'

'When?' Flora stretched up and pressed a kiss against the corner of his mouth before falling back from him again, prevented from staying close by the size of her stomach.

'As soon as possible.' His sapphire-blue eyes stared down into hers with flagrant anticipation. 'I love you... I can't wait to marry you.'

'But I'm...*huge!*' she lamented.

'And supposed to be lying down and resting,' he reminded her in a tone of suppressed urgency, angling her in the direction of the stairs.

Still in shock from having all her dreams come true at one and the same time, Flora allowed him to help her onto the bed and slip off her shoes. She admired her gorgeous ring. She admired Angelo and she smiled sunnily up at him. 'I love you too,' she said belatedly. 'I've been madly in love with you for months.'

'A fine way you have of showing it, *querida mia*!'

Angelo teased, folding down on the bed behind her and easing her into the possessive circle of his arms. 'I was terrified you were going to move out as soon as the babies were born.'

'While I was terrified of moving out because I wouldn't have been able to see you every day any more,' Flora confided. 'I also assumed that you were seeing other women.' She twisted her copper head round to squint at him, her anxiety palpable. *'Did you?'*

'No, I'm yours lock, stock and barrel, *enamorada mia*. I'm definitely a one-woman man,' Angelo confided, his eyes bright with tenderness as he spread big gentle hands across the proud swell of her stomach. 'There's been nobody else in my life and there never will be now.'

His quiet confidence on that score touched her deep. Happiness engulfed her and she covered his hands with hers, looking forward to the day when they could make love again and experience that very special intimacy and pleasure. But the amount of love she could feel in him was sufficient to warm and inspire her.

'I'll marry you as soon as it can be arranged,' she told him softly, stroking the strong male fingers beneath her own. 'Because I can't imagine my life without you, either.'

'And from now on,' Angelo murmured with rich satisfaction, 'I sleep in here with you wrapped in my arms. Do you realise that we've never slept the night through together?'

'Hmm…' Flora framed sleepily, finding that happiness and the amount of heat his big powerful body put out were combining to make her feel incredibly drowsy. That was one wish she could grant him right there and then.

Two years after that night, Flora scanned her reflection critically in the cheval mirror. The green evening dress with the hand-embroidered and beaded bodice had cost a fortune, but that particular colour did seem to give her a positive glow. The figure-fitting contours also made the most of the sleek toned curves that she had worked hard in the gym to recapture after she had given birth.

For the occasion of the charity ball Angelo held in his home every year, her husband had got the family jewels out to deck her from head to toe. She wore the magnificent diamond tiara, necklace and earrings that had once belonged to his mother and the flash of fire that accompanied her every move as the fine jewels caught the light made her feel wonderfully opulent.

'You look breathtaking…'

Flora spun round, her dress rustling with the movement, to focus on the male who had just entered. Her heart in her eyes, she smiled warmly. 'Are they all asleep?'

'Of course,' Angelo countered with more than a little self-satisfaction.

'I don't believe you. I bet they're climbing out of their cots right this minute,' Flora contended with maternal pessimism.

She adored her sons, but Joris, Rip and Hendrik were very lively little boys and getting them to sleep at night was a challenge. Their sister, Mariska, whom Angelo and Flora had officially adopted the previous year, did what she could to keep her brothers in line, but when the three twenty-two-month-old toddlers worked as a team they could be a real headache to keep under control.

'The boys are tired out tonight. Anke and Berna did a great job using up their surplus energy today. Señora van Zaal, you *do* look breathtaking.' Angelo repeated the compliment in a low husky growl and matched it by closing a hand to her wrist to tug her to him.

Flora pulled free again and raised her hands. 'Mind the make-up and the hair!'

'I don't want you so fancy that I can't touch you, *enamorada mia*,' Angelo confessed.

'Well, you will keep on throwing these swanky charity dos,' Flora teased, revelling in the electric-blue heat of his hungry possessive gaze.

She sidestepped her husband to speed down the corridor and go into Mariska's bedroom, where she removed the story books piled up on the bed so that they wouldn't fall during the night and wake the little girl. Julie's daughter was a happy, intelligent child with a lovely gentleness to her nature. She had welcomed the arrival of her three boisterous little brothers and loved being a big sister.

Joris, Rip and Hendrik had been born by C-section when Flora was thirty-three weeks along and the newborns had spent their earliest days in hospital. Rip, the smallest of three, had suffered some breathing difficulties at first but had surmounted his problems and was now the same size as his brothers. Anke had gained a backup in Berna, a second nanny to lighten her load, although Flora spent a great deal of time with her children. In truth, with four young and lively children in need of care and attention there was always plenty of work to be done.

That night's benefit was again in aid of brain-damaged children, the charity which lay closest to Angelo's heart. When Flora had finally got around to asking Angelo who Katja was, she had uncovered a tragic story. Katja had been one of Angelo's schoolmates. At the age of sixteen she had been knocked down by a car and ever since then had lived in a care home because she now had the mental capacities of a young child. After Katja's parents died, it was Angelo who had taken overall responsibility for her continuing care. Angelo visited Katja most weeks, often bringing her one of the animal jigsaws she enjoyed. Having accompanied him on several of those visits, Flora loved Angelo all the more for his generous heart.

The past two years had been action-packed and very happy for Flora, who had gained a good deal of confidence since her marriage. She had fond memories of their small private wedding at the old church that lay only a kilometre from Huis van Zaal. It hadn't mattered to her that she had worn an ivory lace maternity frock or that she'd had to return to bed to rest soon after the ceremony. What had really mattered was the love and tenderness she'd recognised in Angelo's eyes when he'd made his vows. When the boys were three months old, they had flown to the Caribbean to enjoy an extended honeymoon. Bleakly aware that she had not resonated with Angelo, Bregitta Etten had ceased her visits and was not missed.

Flora paused in the doorway of the nursery where her sons were fast asleep. Unusually, there wasn't a sound from the line of cots. She could see the three little dark heads, which were so rarely still during the day, unless they were plotting some mischief. She called Skipper out from below the nearest cot where he would happily have remained for the night had he been allowed to do so, for he adored the boys.

'I have a very beautiful wife and four wonderful kids,' Angelo pronounced from behind her, closing his arms round his wife to slowly turn her round to face him. 'I'm a very lucky man.'

Flora gazed up into his sapphire-blue eyes and her heart raced in reaction. He never got any less gorgeous, she savoured, and she began to stretch up.

'Make-up…hair, *enamorada mia*,' Angelo reminded her teasingly before her cherry-tinted lips could connect with his and wreak havoc with her carefully groomed appearance.

Her eyes glinted at the crack for, as he had once accurately remarked, they were both equally fond of having the last word. 'Later…' she whispered in a tone of feminine promise and had the very great pleasure of seeing sensuality meld with impatience in the lean, darkly handsome face that she could read so much better now.

'Later…' Angelo husked in sexy agreement, running a playful forefinger down from the pulse flickering at her collarbone to the tiny shadowy valley showing between her small high breasts. Her mouth running dry, she had to gasp for breath.

Angelo curved a hand to her spine to guide her downstairs in readiness to greet their guests. 'I suppose you know I'm crazy about you.'

'But I like it when you tell me.' Flora dealt him a provocative smile from below her lashes. 'After all, I'm totally in love with you.'

'Maybe just one kiss,' Angelo muttered thickly at the head of the stairs.

A wicked glint in her green eyes, Flora pulled away with a victorious giggle and raced downstairs with the full skirt of her dress flying like an emerald banner and Skipper tagging her heels...

Harlequin *Presents*

Coming Next Month

from **Harlequin Presents® EXTRA.** Available April 12, 2011.

#145 PICTURE OF INNOCENCE
Jacqueline Baird
Italian Temptation!

#146 THE PROUD WIFE
Kate Walker
Italian Temptation!

#147 SURF, SEA AND A SEXY STRANGER
Heidi Rice
One Hot Fling

#148 WALK ON THE WILD SIDE
Natalie Anderson
One Hot Fling

Coming Next Month

from **Harlequin Presents®.** Available April 26, 2011.

#2987 JESS'S PROMISE
Lynne Graham
Secretly Pregnant...Conveniently Wed!

#2988 THE RELUCTANT DUKE
Carole Mortimer
The Scandalous St. Claires

#2989 NOT A MARRYING MAN
Miranda Lee

#2990 THE UNCLAIMED BABY
Melanie Milburne
The Sabbatini Brothers

#2991 A BRIDE FOR KOLOVSKY
Carol Marinelli

#2992 THE HIGHEST STAKES OF ALL
Sara Craven
The Untamed

HPCNM0411

REQUEST YOUR
FREE BOOKS!

Harlequin *Presents*

PASSION GUARANTEED SEDUCTION

2 FREE NOVELS PLUS
2 FREE GIFTS!

YES! Please send me 2 FREE Harlequin Presents® novels and my 2 FREE gifts (gifts are worth about $10). After receiving them, if I don't wish to receive any more books, I can return the shipping statement marked "cancel." If I don't cancel, I will receive 6 brand-new novels every month and be billed just $4.05 per book in the U.S. or $4.74 per book in Canada. That's a saving of at least 15% off the cover price! It's quite a bargain! Shipping and handling is just 50¢ per book in the U.S. and 75¢ per book in Canada.* I understand that accepting the 2 free books and gifts places me under no obligation to buy anything. I can always return a shipment and cancel at any time. Even if I never buy another book, the two free books and gifts are mine to keep forever.

106/306 HDN FC55

Name _____ (PLEASE PRINT) _____

Address _____ Apt. # _____

City _____ State/Prov. _____ Zip/Postal Code _____

Signature (if under 18, a parent or guardian must sign) _____

Mail to the **Reader Service:**
IN U.S.A.: P.O. Box 1867, Buffalo, NY 14240-1867
IN CANADA: P.O. Box 609, Fort Erie, Ontario L2A 5X3

Not valid for current subscribers to Harlequin Presents books.

**Are you a current subscriber to Harlequin Presents books
and want to receive the larger-print edition?
Call 1-800-873-8635 or visit www.ReaderService.com.**

* Terms and prices subject to change without notice. Prices do not include applicable taxes. Sales tax applicable in N.Y. Canadian residents will be charged applicable taxes. Offer not valid in Quebec. This offer is limited to one order per household. All orders subject to credit approval. Credit or debit balances in a customer's account(s) may be offset by any other outstanding balance owed by or to the customer. Please allow 4 to 6 weeks for delivery. Offer available while quantities last.

Your Privacy—The Reader Service is committed to protecting your privacy. Our Privacy Policy is available online at www.ReaderService.com or upon request from the Reader Service.

We make a portion of our mailing list available to reputable third parties that offer products we believe may interest you. If you prefer that we not exchange your name with third parties, or if you wish to clarify or modify your communication preferences, please visit us at www.ReaderService.com/consumerchoice or write to us at Reader Service Preference Service, P.O. Box 9062, Buffalo, NY 14269. Include your complete name and address.

*With an evil force hell-bent on destruction,
two enemies must unite to find a truth that turns
all-too-personal when passions collide.*

*Enjoy a sneak peek in Jenna Kernan's next installment
in her original* TRACKER *series, GHOST STALKER,
available in May, only from Harlequin Nocturne.*

"**W**ho are you?" he snarled.

Jessie lifted her chin. "Your better."

His smile was cold. "Such arrogance could only come from a Niyanoka."

She nodded. "Why are you here?"

"I don't know." He glanced about her room. "I asked the birds to take me to a healer."

"And they have done so. Is that *all* you asked?"

"No. To lead them away from my friends." His eyes fluttered and she saw them roll over white.

Jessie straightened, preparing to flee, but he roused himself and mastered the momentary weakness. His eyes snapped open, locking on her.

Her heart hammered as she inched back.

"Lead who away?" she whispered, suddenly afraid of the answer.

"The ghosts. Nagi sent them to attack me so I would bring them to her."

The wolf must be deranged because Nagi did not send ghosts to attack living creatures. He captured the evil ones after their death if they refused to walk the Way of Souls, forcing them to face judgment.

"Her? The healer you seek is also female?"

"Michaela. She's Niyanoka, like you. The last Seer of Souls and Nagi wants her dead."

Jessie fell back to her seat on the carpet as the possibility of this ricocheted in her brain. Could it be true?

"Why should I believe you?" But she knew why. His black aura, the part that said he had been touched by death. Only a ghost could do that. But it made no sense.

Why would Nagi hunt one of her people and why would a Skinwalker want to protect her? She had been trained from birth to hate the Skinwalkers, to consider them a threat.

His intent blue eyes pinned her. Jessie felt her mouth go dry as she considered the impossible. Could the trickster be speaking the truth? Great Mystery, what evil was this?

She stared in astonishment. There was only one way to find her answers. But she had never even met a Skinwalker before and so did not even know if they dreamed.

But if he dreamed, she would have her chance to learn the truth.

Look for GHOST STALKER by Jenna Kernan,
available May only from Harlequin Nocturne,
wherever books and ebooks are sold.